Jordan
Stryker

Jordan Stryker
BIONIC AGENT

MALCOLM ROSE

USBORNE

First published in the UK in 2010 by Usborne Publishing Ltd., Usborne House,
83-85 Saffron Hill, London EC1N 8RT, England. www.usborne.com

Copyright © Malcolm Rose, 2010

The right of Malcolm Rose to be identified as the author of this work has been
asserted by him in accordance with the Copyright, Designs and Patents Act,
1988.

Cover illustration by Daniel Atanasov at folioart.co.uk

The name Usborne and the devices ♀ ⊕ are Trade Marks of Usborne
Publishing Ltd.

A CIP catalogue record for this book is available from the British Library.

ISBN 9781409509752 JFM MJJASOND/10 95840

Printed in Reading, Berkshire, UK.

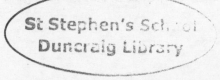

1 EXPLOSION

"I need to speak to the Prime Minister."

"He's asleep."

"Wake him up, then."

"Can't it wait till morning?"

"No. Put him on the phone now."

"But..."

"It's an emergency."

"Can't I...?"

"No, you can't. Only the PM can give the go-ahead to

evacuate north Kent and south Essex. And give it right now. Not in half an hour, not in the morning. Now."

As soon as his secretary switched on the bedroom light and called his name, the Prime Minister was alert. Being woken in the dead of night meant only one thing. There was a crisis. The chill thought snapped his brain into gear at once. He threw back the duvet and got up. Leaving his wife, he grabbed his dressing gown and said, "What is it?"

"The Head of MI5. She wouldn't deal with me. Something about evacuating the south-east."

In the office, the Prime Minister took the secure phone. "Yes?"

"I don't have time for a full briefing, Prime Minister. You're aware of the wreck of the *Richard Montgomery* in the Thames Estuary, aren't you?"

The PM shuddered. "Yes. The one with the explosives." It was a difficult and costly challenge that the Department of Transport was too nervous to tackle.

In 1944, the SS *Richard Montgomery* was delivering 1400 tonnes of explosives for the war effort when strong winds pushed it onto a sandbank in the River Thames.

It broke its back. The wreck with its deadly cargo had remained there ever since, two-and-a-half kilometres from Sheerness and eight kilometres from Southend. No government had risked moving it or making it safe because one small mistake could trigger the bombs. If that happened, the blast would be one of the world's biggest non-nuclear explosions.

"We're facing an imminent threat," the Head of MI5 said. "There's an unauthorized boat moored to one of the warning buoys. The Port of London Authority has got it on radar. We think a diver's gone down..."

"Whose boat is it?"

"We don't know," she replied.

"Would anyone go there for any reason other than making trouble?"

"Not that I can think of. And the boat's ignored radio warnings to move away from the wreck. Whoever it is, they're not answering communications and they haven't issued any demands."

The PM muttered a curse. "What are the options?"

"Very few. We can't engage the boat militarily. Any disturbance could set the bombs off. As you know, they're unstable. I have the army, Kent and Essex Police, the Marine and Coastguard Agency, Medway Ports, and the emergency services on standby. I suggest we evacuate the area, up to three kilometres inland. And get as many as possible away from the gas and oil terminals around the Isle of Grain and Canvey Island. If they go up, it doesn't bear thinking about."

"How many people is that?"

"Forty thousand. Maybe more."

The Prime Minister made an instant decision. "Go ahead. Keep me informed."

In the semi-darkness, the three rusted masts poking out of the water looked like sinister church crosses. The same notice had been attached to each one:

DANGER
UNEXPLODED AMMUNITION
DO NOT APPROACH OR BOARD THIS WRECK
By order

Water lapped gently – as if waiting for something to happen. Tied to a buoy, a small deserted motorboat bobbed around menacingly. Now and again, a stream of bubbles rose and broke the surface.

* * *

Ben Smith couldn't sleep. He stood by his bedroom window in Lower Stoke and gazed towards the Thames Estuary. The fields in front of him were never truly dark. To his right the oil refinery was bathed in nightlights and straight ahead the Isle of Grain gas terminal was lit up like a giant fairground. Tapping out a perfect rhythm with his fingers on the windowsill, Ben thought about the Goss family and Amy Goss in particular.

Earlier in the evening, he'd met Amy in their usual place, between the silos in the messy farm at the end of the track leading from Grain Road. That was their secret place. They'd sat together on the earth among the grey containers that looked like eight huge, upright tubes of toothpaste. Daylight had begun to fade. In the shadows of the large cylinders, it was virtually dark. Anyone walking within a few metres would never have known that the two thirteen-year-olds were there. They would not be seen together. They were safe.

"Who do you think did it?" Amy had whispered even though there was no one to hear them.

She was talking about the biggest thing to happen at school this term. Someone had stolen their science teacher's mobile phone. And, Ben guessed, she wanted to talk about it because she thought she'd get the blame. Mr. Bool was a big man – more like a bouncer than a teacher – and he always looked grouchy. He'd been increasingly tetchy recently. His accusing eyes had turned towards Amy when he'd announced the theft. A lot of the kids had sniggered and eyeballed her as well. But Ben knew Amy better. He hadn't believed for a second that she was the culprit. "Well," he'd said, "I know why everyone looked at you. Your dad's behind ninety-nine point nine per cent of the crime on this planet..."

"Huh! Exaggeration or what?" Amy had replied. "But he's the criminal mastermind of Lower Stoke for sure."

"And Medway."

"Maybe."

"And Kent."

"Well..."

"Everyone knows it. Even the police."

"They haven't arrested him."

Ben had smiled. "Mum says she knows exactly what your dad's up to. It's just that she hasn't got proof."

"That's her problem."

"Yeah, but that's why she always tells me to keep clear of the Gosses."

"And I'm told not to mix with you," Amy had replied with a giggle. "Cop families aren't to be trusted – to put it mildly."

As always, Amy looked quirky and cute. Today, it had been the combination of beanie hat and painted fingernails with hummingbird transfers that had caught Ben's eye.

Perhaps it was the danger of being with Amy that made their friendship irresistible. If Mr. Goss ever found out, he could make life very uncomfortable – even painful – for Ben. And for Amy. If Ben's mum found out, she'd ground him for ever. Detective Sergeant Smith's son could not be seen with a Goss.

As usual, Ben had begun to drum a complicated rhythm with his fingers on one of the metal struts at the base of the grain silo and Amy had begun to complain. "I still don't know how you do that. It's really clever, but it drives me mad."

"Sorry," Ben remembered saying. Even though he hadn't wanted to leave Amy, he'd scrambled to his feet. "It's getting late. If I'm not back for dinner, Mum'll send half the Force out looking for me."

Amy had got up as well. "Dad would just put some heavies on the street and they'd beat people up until someone said, 'I saw her go that way with Ben Smith.'"

Poking his head out from behind the silo, Ben had reported, "All clear."

As they'd walked back down the track together, he'd

said quietly, "Anyway, I know you didn't nick Bool's phone."

She had gazed into his face and nodded. "Good."

"I know because your mobile's much classier than his. Why would you nick it?"

In response, she'd thumped him on the arm.

They'd split up as soon as they neared Grain Road. They always left the shadows separately.

Now, it was the middle of the night and Ben still felt wide awake. Facing the window with the curtains open, he rubbed his right arm where she'd hit him. The bruise was probably still there. He smiled because it was a friendly bruise.

It was quiet and calm as a ship, carrying 125,000 cubic metres of liquefied natural gas to the terminal on the Isle of Grain, made its way slowly along the dredged channel 200 metres from the wreck of the *Richard Montgomery*. The true size of *Ocean Courage* wasn't clear in the gloom but its lights hinted that it was as big as a village. There were only five small craft in the estuary and they buzzed around the lumbering monster like midges.

Without warning, the peace ended.

In a massive explosion, a vast column of seawater,

mud, metal and munitions erupted from around the *Richard Montgomery* and shot into the sky. The instant mushroom was hundreds of metres wide and over two kilometres high. Unexploded bombs from the cargo hold were hurled across the entire area. Almost at once, every single pane of glass in the town of Sheerness shattered. The Animal Breeding Station on the seafront at the end of Beach Street took the full force of the blast and crumbled.

One of the airborne bombs crashed right through *Ocean Courage*, another pierced a gas holding tank on the Isle of Grain, and three hit the oil terminal. All of them exploded immediately.

The night was replaced by giant splashes of bright light as each blast triggered another and then another. *Ocean Courage* became a floating inferno. Its crew of thirty had no time to save themselves. Its supply of liquefied gas sent giant yellow spheres high into the sky.

As the enormous pillar of water plunged back down into the estuary, a four-metre wave radiated outwards, heading with devastating force for the coastlines of Medway and Essex. It rocked the blazing *Ocean Courage*, swept over the smaller vessels and sank them. The shock of the explosions caused an earth tremor that travelled through the estuary clay and shook every building up to three kilometres inland. Some wobbled, several collapsed.

A supertanker discharging its supply of oil under the floodlights of Canvey Island terminal blew up in a mass of searing yellow flame and black smoke. The nightshift workers who hadn't yet been evacuated didn't stand a chance. The ammunition stored at Canvey Arms Factory ignited. The detonation flattened the factory and burning fragments shot into the sky like malicious fireworks. Huge oil storage tanks exploded in sequence along the Essex estuary. The deafening blasts could be heard from four counties.

The area would have been hit very hard even if the bombs stored in the *Richard Montgomery* had been the only source of destruction. But the arms factory, the supertanker, the oil containers, and the passing *Ocean Courage* made a far more lethal cocktail. Metal shards flew like bullets across Southend and the other coastal towns. The authorities' attempts to get the residents away only made it worse. People were on the streets and in vehicles when the lethal missiles arrived and the shock wave turned windows into weapons.

The emergency services had put all their effort into clearing the large centres of population. The smaller places had no warning.

In Lower Stoke, just a short distance across the fields from the gas terminal, Ben Smith was by his bedroom window. When the gasworks exploded, his house was the first to feel the power of the blast. Immediately, the roof above his head ripped away. Tiles and beams came down. His window splintered and showered him with glass. He didn't even have time to cry out. He was tossed across the room along with bricks, plaster, his bed and electronic drum kit. His head smacked sickeningly against something solid. Then he was falling because there was no longer a floor beneath his feet.

The shock wave caused a massive change in air pressure. It ruptured his lungs, eardrums and bowels.

Ben knew he was badly injured. He'd seen his right arm being torn away from his shoulder. He was aware of warm blood. Lots of it. But he felt no pain. Perhaps it was so intense that his body had shut down. He had already moved on to a calmer place. Yet his eyes remained open.

The firefighter didn't need to look closely into the ruins. The state of the bodies told her all she needed to know. The explosion had wiped out an entire family. She said into the microphone attached to her uniform, "Fourteen

Shepherds Way – with parts of sixteen, I think – Lower Stoke. Just awful. Too close to the blast."

"Fourteen Shepherds Way is a priority address," Control said through her earpiece. "A police officer's house. DS Smith. According to records, she wasn't on duty. She was probably in bed."

"I'm sorry. It's a war zone down here. No one's alive."

But, as Debbie turned to leave, the boy's body caught her attention. He was so young. A teenager, she guessed. His skin was as deathly grey as the rest of his family. There was no movement, no sign of breathing, but his eyes were open and they didn't have the usual clouded appearance.

"Just a second," she said, clambering over the debris.

"What is it?" Control asked. "Do you want medical assistance?"

"I don't think so." She kneeled by the boy and felt his left wrist. His right arm was completely missing. Glass from a shattered window had slashed and speared several parts of his body. Even his eyes had been pierced. The back of his skull had smashed against the remains of the brick wall. His brain had probably been severely damaged and he'd lost a huge volume of blood. His arm was still warm and soft but there was no pulse. She reached out and felt his pale neck. Nothing.

"False alarm," she told Control. "It's a boy. He's dead. I just hope he went quickly."

"Move on," said Control.

Even though she believed no one could survive such awful injuries, Debbie did not abandon the boy straight away. With the back of her hand, she stroked his unresponsive bloodless cheek. At his age, he would have had so much to look forward to. She shook her head with desperation, maybe with defiance.

She knew that medical teams were stretched to breaking point treating the injured. They didn't have time for hopeless cases. But something inside her refused to accept the boy's fate. Maybe it was because of those bloodshot eyes. She could imagine some lingering consciousness behind them. "No," she said into the tiny microphone. "I want medical backup."

"What? Do you have signs of life?"

No pulse, no breathing, no movement. No ordinary human would have the strength and willpower to survive an ordeal like this. But she sensed that this boy was different. She sensed some sort of determination about him. She knew that Control wouldn't send help if she was honest, so she lied. "I thought he just moved."

"Are you sure?"

Deborah Metland swallowed uncomfortably. She had to be crazy but her instinct told her that what she was doing was right. It told her that this boy was more than ordinary. "Yes. Quick. Get a resuscitation team in here."

2 CEMETERY

Pumped full of someone else's blood, Ben lay in a coma
in the Intensive Care Unit of The Whittington Hospital.
For a week, he was also pumped full of antibiotics to
fight infection, and adrenalin to keep his blood pressure
above zero. No one gave him a chance of surviving.
Then, against all the odds, he showed signs of regaining
consciousness and he was pumped full of morphine to
make the pain bearable. At first, he was barely aware
of his surroundings but, once he was out of immediate

danger of dying, he was moved to a high dependency room.

Amazing the medics with his will to live, he suffered long periods of confusion and vague wakefulness before he began to make sense of the world and his injuries. Yet he was determined.

He was especially determined to move, to live without tubes attached, to go to the bathroom on his own and to confront his condition. Two nurses were with him when he first manoeuvred his legs over the edge of the bed. Feeling like a baby about to become a toddler, he looked down at the floor and wondered if he could walk. He also wondered how painful it would be. If he fell, the nurse on his left would clutch his arm. He didn't know what the nurse on the right would do. There wasn't much for her to grab. But he did it. He didn't fall. He took a few steps – as far as the tubes and monitors would allow. For a few seconds, he was independent. He was in control of himself.

As soon as he was capable of staying on his feet for a brief period with the aid of a walking frame, he stood in front of a full-length mirror in his private room. He couldn't see very well but, even though his doctors had warned him about his appearance, he was horrified by the damage that an explosion could inflict on a human being. What he saw in the mirror was a terrible and torn imposter. It was a rag doll that had been ripped to pieces and sewn back together again. But it wasn't even complete. Whoever had stitched the cruel figure had not found all of the pieces. And the image brought tears to his eyes.

He was bruised, battered, cut and scarred. He was a mass of swellings, scabs, stitches and dressings. Missing his right arm and ear, he was also lopsided. His eyesight was clouded, unfocused and lacked colour. Short-sighted – anything beyond a few metres was washed out in a hazy grey – he didn't stand a chance of identifying anything moving rapidly. His hearing was poor. The sounds of the hospital were muffled. Apparently, a part of his brain that handled hearing, sight and smell had been mangled in the Thames Estuary explosion.

His mouth was cut and distorted. His cheek had been ripped away. Part of his shaved head was still bandaged. The rest was covered with blisters, bumps and blackened blood. His whole head seemed to be a different shape, especially at the back where he couldn't quite see. He knew that his skull was broken there, though. That's why he'd been given a boxing helmet. It was supposed to protect the fracture from further damage if he fell over or walked into a wall. Tottering right up to the glass, he peered closely at his eyes. He couldn't make out what was wrong with them, but they didn't look right.

Ben had unseen scars as well. Mental scars. When a doctor had managed to make him understand what had happened to his family, he'd wished he'd been allowed to die beside them. His mum, dad, big brother and sister. Gone in an instant.

His mum used to say with a smile, "When I'm past it, just take me out and shoot me. Get it over with. Let me bow out with a bit of dignity." It was illegal, of course. But, even though she was a police officer, she kind of meant it. Perhaps a massive dose of morphine had been more on her mind than a gun. In Ben's case, though, the morphine was not meant to take life away. It made life tolerable by killing his pain.

There was one sentence he kept hearing. *You're lucky to be alive*. All the doctors and nurses said the same thing. It was the first sentence he remembered hearing when he'd come round. He couldn't hear properly, but he'd heard that. Lucky! He didn't feel lucky. He felt incredible pain. That's all.

Standing in front of the mirror, he wondered what he'd be called. The patchwork boy. The orphan. The scarecrow. The invalid. Where was the luck in that?

And what about all the things he used to do with his

right arm? Playing tennis, drumming, throwing, writing, supporting his own weight, tapping a keypad, punching and everything else. What about all those simple things – like getting dressed and eating – that required two hands? Exhausted, he shuffled back to bed like a ninety-year-old.

Yet, over the coming days, somehow, he summoned the strength and courage to carry on.

As soon as The Whittington had made him stable and treated the worst of his injuries, Ben had his first visitor. Confined to his room in the north London hospital, he was pleased to hear that someone had come to see him. Maybe some relative had heard what had happened and come to take care of him. Maybe Grandma and Granddad had flown in from their home in Australia. Maybe it was Amy Goss. He hoped it was Amy. He needed to talk to someone. But his visitor wasn't a friend or relative.

An immensely tall and skinny but authoritative figure stepped out of the fog of his damaged eyesight. When the man came closer, Ben realized that he'd never seen him before.

"It's Ben Smith, isn't it?" he said in a loud voice. Obviously, he knew that Ben was partly deaf.

Ben nodded. "Yes."

"I heard about you – and your circumstances. You're an extraordinary boy. These injuries would've been too much for most people, but your body's decided to carry on. I'm Angel, by the way."

"Oh." Not Dr. Angel, Mr. Angel or Angel Something. Just Angel.

"I run a specialist unit up the road."

"Specializing in what?"

"Well, one thing I can do is help someone like you," Angel replied. He almost shouted. "Artificial limbs, the very best in plastic surgery, getting your brain and eyes to function properly again, and coming to terms with a new life. It's about enhancing a damaged body, making you stronger than you were before."

Ben liked the sound of being stronger than before, but he couldn't believe that it would ever happen. He imagined he was beyond repair. "What's this unit called?"

"It's got a name," Angel said, "but I'd rather not talk about it here when anyone could just walk in on us. Don't worry, though. It's all been cleared with the hospital. They've given me your details and I've set up a medical room especially for you."

Ben frowned. It was a strange response from a strange man. There again, Ben was going through a strange period. It was a time when doctors and nurses ruled his life. Apparently, it was a time when a weird man could come into his room and take control over his treatment.

A mother and father were made for moments like this. A mother or father would say, "Hey, what's going on here? Who are you, exactly? What are your qualifications? Tell me more." A mother or father would check everything and then say, "Yes, Ben. It's for the best. This Angel's going to help you." But Ben didn't have a mother or father any more. He was on his own. He had to make his own decisions.

"What do I have to do?" Ben asked.

Angel smiled. "Not a lot. I'll get one of the doctors – a friend of mine – to come in and talk to you about it. Make sure you're happy with what's happening. Then the hospital discharges you into my care. That's it. A drive up the hill and we're there in five minutes." He shrugged. "If it doesn't work out, you come back here, but I don't think you'll want to do that."

Ben thought about it for a moment and then said, "Okay."

"Good decision," Angel replied. "I'll get things moving."

The mysterious Angel didn't waste time. The next day, Ben saw the outside world for the first time since the explosion. But not for long. The car went up the busy hill to Highgate Village, and turned left into the narrow road called Swain's Lane. Suddenly, it didn't feel like London any more. The car crawled along, past a large radio mast, avoiding the tourists heading for Waterlow Park and Highgate Cemetery. Within a minute, it pulled up outside a large house which backed onto the lane. The tall wall that separated its garden from Swain's Lane was topped with spikes and two security cameras scanned the area.

Angel got out, tapped a code into a keypad by the garage and then pushed open the steel door. "Don't be put off by the back. Come up to the living room. It's superb."

Ben hoped no one was looking. He looked stupid in the protective boxing helmet. Then he went to grab the door with the hand he no longer had. He adjusted his position so that he could hold it open with his single crutch instead. It closed behind him with a clunk that even he could hear was solid and secure.

Tired after walking up one short flight of stairs, Ben gasped as he walked into the large, sparsely furnished living room. One entire side was made of glass panels and it overlooked Highgate Cemetery. He was immediately drawn to the massive window and the view of stone crosses, plinths and headstones among the vegetation. It took him a few seconds to realize that the bizarre, fuzzy shapes like frozen zombies were bushes growing up and over some of the monuments. He couldn't make out the more distant trees and the bobbing heads of a group of visitors taking the guided tour of the graveyard. They were lost in the permanent haze of his feeble vision.

"There's a veranda above us that's got an even better view. Good for recuperation." Angel turned towards Ben and, sensing his frustration, added, "Your vision's one of the first things we'll sort out."

Ben was puzzled. The building appeared to be a large, modern yet ordinary home within Highgate Cemetery. "You said this was a specialized unit or something. It's just a house. A house in a graveyard!"

"Yes," Angel replied, "but with some additional features that aren't immediately obvious. You'll see. Right now, though, you're looking pale. You need rest and I want my doctor to look you over in the medical room. There's a lift down to it."

"A lift? Down?"

"That's one of the unusual features. Underground rooms."

"What is this place? Not a hospital or a surgery."

"It's very private but still in the heart of London. It's

called Unit Red. We'll talk about it once you're settled."

"My painkillers are wearing off."

Angel nodded sympathetically. "Come on. I'll show you your bedroom and then get the doctor to fix you up."

Ben's bedroom was up one more floor. A small airy room – clinically clean – with a view over the sleepy cemetery. He opened the wardrobe door and noticed a good range of brand new clothes. After his house had been destroyed, he didn't expect to see his own gear, but he became distressed straight away because the neatly arranged wardrobe reminded him of everything he'd lost. "These aren't mine!"

"I'm sorry," said Angel. "They are all your size, though."

Every shoe stored at the bottom of the wardrobe had Velcro fastenings. That was because human beings needed two hands to tie laces.

Ben flopped onto the edge of the bed and winced at the pain of his sudden movement. Head bowed, he muttered, "I've got nothing. No clothes, no family, no photos, no phone. No possessions at all. No friends. Not even a home. Nothing."

"I can get you whatever you need," Angel told him.

"That's not the point, is it? Can you bring my family back?"

"No."

"What about my friend, Amy? I want to see her."

Angel shook his head. "Now's not the right time. Come on." Angel guided him towards the door. "Let's have you checked over."

Ben needed the support of a crutch to keep him upright, but his body was so pathetic, he could manage only one. The lift took them down to a windowless corridor with a series of doors. Knowing that the house had gravestones right outside, Ben realized that these hidden rooms must lie alongside the dead. On the other side of the walls had to be the decomposed remains of corpses. Ben wasn't sure if that was freaky or comforting. The occupants of the burial ground could cast an eerie shadow on the house or they might watch over it. He hoped that living next to them would be like having the protection of ancestors.

He hesitated before he went into the medical room. Looking like a dentist's surgery with a high-tech chair and all sorts of modern gadgetry, it made him feel anxious and reassured at the same time. Clearly, the room had been prepared for him in advance because the walls were plastered with close-ups of his wounds, X-ray images and brain scans. He recognized some of them from the hospital. The medical mural was the story of his infirmity: a shattered shoulder, a fractured skull, and a black hole in the marbled grey of his brain like a terrible storm cloud. Apparently, Unit Red – whoever they were – already knew him inside out.

Over the coming weeks, Ben spent a lot of time in the medical room, mere metres away from the skeletons of Highgate Cemetery. He saw doctors, surgeons, an optician, a physiotherapist, even engineers, technicians and computer experts to mend his broken body. And there was a psychiatrist. She wanted to mend his broken mind – to help him overcome the mental trauma of losing his family and parts of his body. Apart from her, they all said the same old phrase – *you're lucky to be alive* – before they set about improving him.

Above them all in the specialist centre was Angel. Unit Red's boss came and went, but he was fond of saying that he would be available every step of the way as Ben learned to live again. He was less fond of explanations. He always avoided talking about the exact nature and purpose of Unit Red.

Outside, the world carried on without Ben. The dead were laid to rest and mourned. The police were investigating the Thames explosion, following a lot of leads, but making no arrests. Most of the ruins on the south Essex and north Kent coasts would be rebuilt.

Some businesses and people would start up again. Many would find it too painful and move away. Confined to the Unit Red headquarters in London, Ben would also be rebuilt.

Sometimes, thoughts of life beyond Highgate Cemetery came to Ben's mind. Usually, they hit him when the pain would not go away or when he couldn't sleep. He ached to know what had happened to Amy and why, according to Angel, it was never the right time to be reunited with friends. He ached to know who had robbed him of his normal life, his friends and family, everything he had. And he ached to know why.

3 TRANSFORMATION

Unit Red's chief surgeon led Ben to the room at the end of the underground corridor. Hesitating by the door, he said, "This is where you'll have the big operations." Going inside, he added, "Sometimes you'll see it. Sometimes you won't. It depends whether you need local or general anaesthetic."

Ben gasped in amazement. He was inside a tiny observation room. Beyond the window was a fully equipped, modern and spotless operating theatre, just like in a hospital.

"It's sealed," the surgeon told him, "to prevent infections. We can't go in without scrubbing up and getting into sterile clothing."

Ben's eyes struggled to focus. He couldn't make out all of the equipment and, even if he could, he wouldn't have recognized most of the high-tech kit. There was a large trolley with electronic gear on each shelf and a long monitor at the top. A giant computer screen and a digital clock were attached to the left-hand wall. There was a cupboard that probably contained horrible things like scalpels, drills and medical saws. Above the operating table were three massive round lights on jointed arms so that they could be moved into any position. There was also a laser. At the head of the bed was a doughnut-shaped ring that would just about encircle a body like a lifebelt. "What's that for?" Ben said, pointing at it.

"Ah. We'll be using that straight away. It's a brain scanner. MRI – magnetic resonance imaging – it's called. I'm going to drill a couple of small holes through your skull – nothing to worry about – and put implants directly into your brain. The scanner will let me see exactly what I'm doing while I'm doing it. And you can talk to me at the same time."

Ben looked horrified. "Talk? Won't you knock me out first?"

"It's better not to. That way, you can tell me if you can see better when I connect your optic nerve to a brain implant. You won't feel any pain. A local anaesthetic will take care of that."

Ben shivered. He thought there was something weird and ghoulish about talking to a surgeon who was fiddling around inside his brain at the time. He didn't want to hear any more. Instead, he tried to get an answer to a question that Angel had sidestepped. He took a deep breath and asked, "What is Unit Red?"

The chief surgeon smiled. "I think I'll let Angel handle that one – when you're ready. My job is just to make you better."

Ben needed several days to recover after every operation. To keep track of them all, he felt as if he should chalk them up on his bedroom wall in the Unit Red building, like a prisoner marking each day in captivity.

His eyes had been fixed. Both irises had been fitted with a tiny camera and an electrode had been attached to the retina of each eye. The signal from the cameras was picked up by the electrodes and fed directly into his optic nerve. The sensory information was handled partly by his brain and partly by an implant, letting him see clearly. More than clearly. He had the best eyesight in the world. And it wasn't just visible light. The cameras worked over a wide wavelength range. He had infrared vision so he could see in the dark and terahertz vision that allowed him to look straight through people's clothes. Except that he hadn't mastered the full scope of his new eyes yet. Until he learned how to cope, he had to put up with the confusing crossover of different wavelengths. He had to put up with the bizarre sensation that warm-blooded beings looked like radioactive aliens. And sometimes they appeared naked.

Even though he now had amazing high-tech eyes, no one would notice unless they came quite close.

The next operation was a big one. It was the first step to giving him a new arm and it meant general anaesthetic and a long recovery. Ben was scared and pleased at the same time. He was fed up with looking odd and ugly, like a teapot without its spout. He was fed up with being unbalanced. Fed up with fighting his instincts to reach out with an arm that was no longer there. Fed up with his slow and hopeless left arm. He longed for a time when eating, showering, dressing and undressing didn't take an age. He wanted something to fill his shirtsleeve. He hated the way that clothes simply hung from his right shoulder and flapped around uselessly, like a flag waving to show everyone his impairment. When the frustrations got to him, he'd go to the gym and take it out on a punchbag, but that didn't really work. He could hit it only with this ineffectual left arm.

One of the doctors peered closely at Ben's stumpy shoulder. "You've healed nicely – to the point where we can start working on it. We're going to implant titanium rods into your remaining bones." She demonstrated angles and directions with her pen. "They'll poke through your skin like bolts and we'll fix your new arm onto them. I know it sounds horrible, but it's simple. Not risky. And, when the arm's on, you won't see the fitting."

Ben turned towards Angel, who stood to one side. "You said the arm's really clever and complicated."

"It is. Fantastic. If you call it advanced technology, you're not doing it justice. It's super-advanced. You're the first person in the world to get this version. You'll love it. You'll be able to do incredible things."

The doctor explained, "The mechanism and electronics are tomorrow's state of the art, but the fitting's just nuts and bolts basically. That's what I meant by calling it simple." She spoke clearly to make sure that Ben could hear. "Where you once had flesh, bone, blood and nerves, you'll have motors, carbon-fibre rods, wires and fancy electronics. But it'll look realistic when we've finished."

"Muscles are good," Angel said, "but what you're going to have will be better. Stronger."

Ben gulped. It sounded like something a superhero in a comic would have. But he would not believe in the transformation until it happened. He also wondered what was in it for Unit Red. Why was the mysterious organization helping him?

He asked, "How will I move this arm?"

Angel pointed towards his head. "With thoughts. I told you it was advanced."

"By the way," the doctor added, "while the surgeon's at it, I'll open up your right leg and put a battery under the skin."

"A battery?"

"Something's got to power all your enhancements," she said.

"What happens when it goes flat? Do you have to...?"

She smiled and shook her head. "No. Once it's in, that's it. It won't go flat. It's rechargeable. It generates electricity from movement. You don't have to do anything extraordinary like jump up and down all the time. Just normal walking around and so on will power your arm, visual system and everything else."

Ben didn't like what he was – hampered by disability – but he also worried about what he was becoming.

Seven months after the explosion, Ben stood in front of a full-length mirror once more. Just for a moment, he had the strange sensation that the glass was a door. A weird boy was outside the room, looking in at him. But he was wrong. The mirror was normal and he was the peculiar boy with the bald head. He lifted his left arm to prove it. His unfamiliar reflection did the same.

This time, he wasn't shocked by the damage. He was astonished by the power of surgery to reconstruct a body. Maybe body was the wrong word. He was part body, part machine. Whoever or whatever he saw in the mirror, it wasn't Ben Smith.

His right arm was a gadget. No matter how clever it was, no matter how many things it could do, it was attached to him and not really part of him. At this stage, the motors, metal rods and joints were visible, but it was going to be encased in super-strong metal and covered with artificial skin. Even that wouldn't convince him it was anything but a gadget. At least it would be well disguised when his transformation was complete. From a distance, other people would not notice that he had a robotic arm.

He put his left hand on his cheek. Pure plastic. One ear had been rebuilt out of silicone. His bald head was covered with scars and odd bumps. Focusing on his eyes, he could see the tiny cameras that almost everyone else would miss. The marks all over his body made him look like a carefully constructed jigsaw.

Apart from his right arm and ear, his body glowed yellowy-red. He knew that no one else would see the shimmering colour. His infrared vision was detecting warmth. His right arm and ear were cold and dead. A lifeless blue colour. The patches of plastic on his face and trunk were a darker red. That was the warmth and life underneath struggling to show through.

Taking him by surprise, Angel came up behind him and said, "Ben Smith died."

He spun round. "What?"

"You look full of regret – in mourning for what you once were."

"Can you blame me?"

"You deal with it by disowning that history."

Ben hesitated. "What do you mean?"

"Like everyone else, you admit that Ben Smith died in the estuary blast. Your friends and relatives have had to come to terms with it. Let him go. You become a different boy. In fact," Angel said, smiling at him, "I know who you are. You're Jordan Stryker. I've got the birth certificate, ID and passport that prove it."

The boy standing in front of the mirror was stunned. Yet it made a kind of sense. The explosion had happened to Ben Smith. It was Ben Smith and his family who'd died. The whole horrible experience belonged to someone else. Someone who no longer existed.

"Jordan Stryker," he muttered. It didn't sound right. It denied everything that had ever happened to him. It separated him from his friends. It separated him from Amy. Yet it eliminated the worst thing that had ever happened to him.

He wanted to start afresh. But it wouldn't be simple and it wouldn't be painless. It would be easier for his altered mouth to get used to saying the name than for his brain to accept and become Jordan Stryker. Even so, he made up his mind to take on the new identity.

"You've been through a lot of operations now," Angel said. "It would've broken most people's spirit. But not you. Your body decided it could take more punishment."

"I didn't always want to live."

"Listen. I did some research on you. You were pretty good at tennis. Do you know how many times you came back from losing sets to win matches?"

"Er... A few times."

"More than a few. It looks to me as if the worse things get, the harder you battle."

"I was bigger and stronger than most of the boys I played against. That's all."

Angel shook his head. "There's more to it than muscles. You have to have something special up here," he said, tapping the side of his head, "not to give up when you're a long way behind. For ordinary mortals, not wanting to carry on is a natural reaction straight after something as traumatic as you've been through, but your body was in no mood to give up. It would've been far easier to die than live but... You're still with us. Anyway, if there was a moment of doubt, it didn't last long and it was that other boy's thinking. Ben Smith. He's gone. You're Jordan and up for it. And I've got more challenges for you."

Jordan grimaced. "Like what?"

"We need to work on your sense of smell. And your hearing. I'm tired of shouting at you."

"You're not shouting."

"No, but you miss a lot. We need to sort that out. That's one reason you've got holes in your head. You need another brain implant. We can do some really clever things with sensory data – on the very edge of today's technology. Tomorrow's technology really. And there's physiotherapy. Lots of it. On top of everything else, you're going to learn how to use your arm. I can't lie to you. It's going to take a long time, but you'll control it by thinking. Just like a real arm. Your nerves will activate... Enough. You'll see."

The first phase of his transformation was complete. He had endured being rebuilt. Now, he had to learn how to use his new body. But Jordan was no wiser about his new life. Angel still hadn't told him what lay at the end of his long treatment.

His time in Unit Red was like a never-ending school day, chopped up into periods. Period 1: learning to keep different regions of the visual spectrum apart. Period 2: pinpointing the exact location of sounds. Period 3: using thoughts to communicate with his brain implants. Period 4: a real lesson with a real tutor. Double period 5-6: the infuriatingly slow training to master the artificial arm. Evening homework: extra arm exercises and physiotherapy. Next day: start all over again. And the next: more of the same.

His life was as splintered as his body. At least his new name was beginning to work. He didn't always feel burdened by a painful past. He was becoming Jordan Stryker, without a past.

Picking up an egg without breaking it was a very easy

task for an arm, hand and fingers. But it was a major undertaking for his robotic replacement. The stupid gadget reached out and, if the artificial fingers managed to encircle an egg without knocking it over, they clenched awkwardly until they crushed it. His bionic right arm didn't know its own strength. It smashed the egg every time. And it did the same to mugs, door handles, remote controls, plates – anything.

Frustrated and annoyed, Jordan raised his false arm and crashed it down on a box of eggs. The eggs shattered, the carton broke and the table underneath collapsed with a huge dent in its top.

Angel laughed. A pleasant laugh, not a cruel jibe. "Hey. Remind me not to shake hands with you. Not yet anyway. I've never seen the medical room splattered with so many eggs. It doesn't matter. I'll put the chickens on overtime."

"Holding an egg!" Jordan cried. "A toddler could do it."

"With a real arm, yes. But you're learning to use something else. It's much more difficult. If it helps you to get angry, though, get angry. It's all good practice. Like a martial arts expert smashing bricks with his bare hands. It's okay."

Jordan had to admit that it felt good to let rip. It

released emotion and reminded him how powerful he'd become.

The nerves in Jordan's shoulder that once controlled his right arm had been attached to chest muscle instead. The muscle was redundant because it no longer had to support and move his arm. Now, when he thought about doing something with his right arm, the chest muscle twitched instead. Sensors in his chest detected the muscle movement and sent a message to the motors in his bionic arm, translating the twitches into arm actions.

To Jordan, it didn't really feel like an arm at all. It felt like a Swiss army knife with different modes for different jobs. And he had to learn how to use them all. Until he lost his real arm, he hadn't appreciated how much it could do. He hadn't realized that a human arm was amazing. But there were compensations in having a robotic one. He would never have been able to crush the table with a real arm. He'd make an awesome boxer.

He'd always been a muscular boy with broad shoulders and a body that looked older than his age. A trainer at the sports centre in Lower Stoke had told him that he could be a great boxer, but he hadn't enjoyed hitting people. He'd decided to hit tennis balls and drums instead.

Jordan applied the brakes to his memory. He was trying not to think about his past. He was trying not to think about having a real arm. He was Jordan Stryker. False arm and false ID included. He had to think only about the present and the future. After all, that was where he'd spend the rest of his life.

He reached out for the next egg. His mechanical fingers clutched at it unsteadily like an old person riddled with arthritis. The fingers snapped shut, the shell splintered and the innards oozed out.

Angel smiled. "You don't give up. That's the important point. I know it seems a long way off, but one day you'll handle eggs without making omelettes *and* smash through bricks. Fiddly jobs and brute force. You'll do both."

Jordan breathed deeply, crossed the narrow lane and went into Waterlow Park opposite. He glanced enviously at the tennis courts and strolled towards Middle Pond. He didn't get so tired now, but he was certainly not in peak condition. The bone at the back of his head had strengthened enough so that it no longer needed the protection of a boxer's helmet. He'd even been able to grow his hair because the chief surgeon had no plans to delve into his brain again.

He'd ceased to feel the weight of the battery in his right leg. He could almost forget it was just under the surface of his skin. Every step of every walk, every run, every leg movement, he was recharging it.

Angel was beside him, claiming that he wanted some fresh air. But Angel was not the sort to walk around aimlessly. He probably realized that Jordan was getting restless as he returned to health and began to function again. Almost certainly, Angel accompanied him to provide an opportunity to talk.

It was plain to Jordan that Unit Red was more than a place to repair and enhance his body. He'd seen more people than the medics, engineers, technicians and tutors who were helping him. As he passed them one-by-one in a corridor, they'd smile, nod and say hello. But they wouldn't say much more. Unit Red wasn't a place where people chatted for fun, it seemed. And there was no one else like him. No one young and no one visibly damaged.

All of the people seemed to report to Angel in a secret room called the bunker. The house was always locked and protected by security cameras. Inside, guards seemed to be on duty permanently.

This time, Jordan was determined to get an answer from Angel. When no one was within earshot, he asked,

"What exactly is Unit Red? It can't be just for patching me up."

Angel nodded as if he'd been expecting the question. "You're right. The medical facilities were designed for a case like yours, though. You're the first. Depending how it goes, there may be others. But we'll fit you with improvements now and again, so we need the best equipment and research. On top of that, we have to take care of our own people if they get hurt."

"Doing what?"

"What can I tell you? Have you heard of MI5?" He could speak softly now. Jordan's hearing was acute. It was superhuman, really.

"You mean spies, James Bond and gadgets."

Angel laughed. "James Bond? That'll be the day. No, this is the real world. Unit Red's like MI5 in a way, but more underground. Everyone's heard of MI5, but no one's heard of Unit Red. Apart from my contacts in various places – like Whittington Hospital and the police. The extra secrecy gives us more flexibility to operate behind the scenes."

Puzzled, Jordan asked, "Operate on what?"

"We're a deeper level of British Intelligence. Officially, we don't exist. The government would deny all knowledge of us. You see, they have to be seen to be playing by the rules. Even MI5 and MI6 are tightly regulated these days. We're as law-abiding as we can be, but we have more freedom because we're under the radar. We take on cases the others couldn't solve and, to get results, sometimes we break the rules. Our targets are terrorists and villains who are beyond normal law."

"You're a super-secret agent."

Angel waited for a young woman with a dog to walk past them. She glanced at Jordan but didn't pay him any particular attention. She didn't realize that he was so special. She didn't notice his false arm and altered eyes.

Eventually, Angel said, "There's a bank robber who's been living in Spain, out of the law's reach, for the last twenty years. He's just been arrested at Gatwick. In the news, the story was that the police tricked him into getting onto a UK plane. Well, they didn't. They can't do things like that. It was us. We can operate undercover in Spain and at airports without notifying the normal authorities. I won't tell you exactly how we got him onto the plane, but a doctor made him think he was seriously ill and needed specialist treatment over here. Another Unit Red agent working on the inside helped him come up with a disguise and false passport for the trip. It was a tidy operation."

"Then what?"

"We made a case against him and handed him over to the police. They tell the press and look good. We stay in the shadows."

"Sounds a bit tame," Jordan replied with a grin.

"It was more nerve-racking than exciting," Angel admitted. "But, believe me, we do excitement as well. And it can be dangerous. That's why my people sometimes need medical facilities that are out of the public eye."

Lowering his voice, Jordan said, "Are you licensed to kill like you-know-who?"

Angel's expression remained serious. "Occasionally it comes to that, but killing's never our first choice."

Jordan looked into Angel's steely face and decided not to take it any further. Unit Red's boss was not the sort of person to be quizzed. He was like a friendly but firm teacher. There was always tension in the air when he was around. Jordan didn't know what sort of behaviour would tip Angel's mood from cheerful to strict – or even to scary – but he sensed that Angel did have a tipping point. He would not always be pleasant and relaxed.

Jordan also wondered about Angel's name. It was probably made up, like Jordan Stryker. Maybe real names were in short supply in Unit Red. Maybe Unit

Red's chief was called Angel because he spent his life chasing devils.

"Is this all there is?" Jordan asked, pointing in the direction of the house. "One place in north London?"

"No. There's a network of houses, but this is the HQ."

"When I was in hospital, you said you'd heard about me and my injuries. How?"

"How did I hear about you?"

Jordan nodded. He knew that sometimes journalists chased ambulances to get bad news stories. He wondered if Angel had also chased an ambulance, looking for someone he could rebuild.

"I have high-level clearance. My computer can get into all sorts of records, including hospital files. When I saw what injuries you'd survived, I knew straight away you were remarkable. I thought I could help. My contact – one of the doctors – did the rest." Angel stopped walking and turned towards him. "What's really bothering you?"

Jordan hesitated and then said, "What's Unit Red got to do with me?"

"You're smart, Jordan. I think you know."

Jordan probably did, but he wanted to be sure. He waited for more.

"Unit Red doesn't exist – officially. And neither do you.

You died. The entire world thinks you died. You and the organization are well matched."

"So?"

"I'm always after people I can trust. Special people. There's no doubting you're more special than most."

It wasn't quite an invitation to become a Unit Red agent. But it wasn't far off.

"We're getting ahead of ourselves." Without warning, Angel turned and strode back towards the house. When Jordan caught up with him, he continued, "I want you to concentrate on getting to grips with your new features. Then, if all's well, we'll talk about it. It's definitely a conversation for the bunker."

And that was it. Jordan would have to be patient.

4 PAYBACK

Jordan curled his lip as he looked at the computer monitor. It was showing a movie of a singing nun surrounded by little kids halfway up a mountain. "What's that?" he cried.

"A clip from *The Sound of Music*," Angel said with a smirk.

"The what?"

"It's a film. My grandma's favourite. Things were different back then. What were you trying to get?"

Jordan sighed. "Music. But not that sort."

"You're nearly there," Angel said. "You thought about the sound of music and you got *The Sound of Music*."

"Yeah, but..."

"Try something else." Angel tapped the computer and said, "In here, I've got a file on someone called Henry Quickfall. It's like his police record. See if you can get it up on screen."

Jordan didn't need a keypad to log on to the computer. He was in wireless contact with Unit Red's network through his latest brain implant. It was called a brain/computer interface or BCI. He'd already learned to think his password into the system. Then the network's resources were his. To get precisely what he wanted, thinking the right thoughts should have been as good as typing a phrase into a search engine. But it wasn't easy.

He concentrated on the name. *Henry Quickfall*. The screen switched to a page posted by Wiltshire County Council. It celebrated the fact that Henry Quickfall had been voted the Cleaner of the Year for two years in succession.

"Is that him?" Jordan asked.

Angel smiled broadly. "No. The Henry Quickfall I know wouldn't win any awards."

"What's he done?"

"He's a militant campaigner. And he lives in Southend, not Wiltshire."

Jordan tried again. *Henry Quickfall. Campaigner. Southend-on-Sea*.

The screen went blank. Two irrelevant images flashed up, too fast to take in. Then Unit Red's file on Henry Quickfall appeared. Like magic.

"There. I knew you could do it," Angel told him.

Jordan was too pleased with his achievement to take in the information on screen. For him, it was enough that he could access it. But he did notice that Quickfall was listed as an animal rights activist and environmental protester. One word caught his eye because it was in capital letters: POPE.

"It's clever, but..."

"What?"

Jordan said, "It's great that I can get online wherever I go but, unless I'm in front of a monitor, I can't see what I've logged on to."

Angel nodded. "I've got my computer people working on that. You know the cameras in your eyes send what they see into your optic nerve via the electrodes at the back of your eyes? Well, when your BCI receives information from the computer, we're working on feeding that to the same electrodes so it'll go into your optic nerve as well. You'll be able to see the pages as if the screen was right in front of you."

"Wow!" There were advantages to having probes inserted through the skull. An online brain was one enhancement that any school kid would wish to have. It would make exams a whole lot easier.

Education was different for Jordan. It was nothing like the schooling of Ben Smith – and every other fourteen-year-old. Ben hadn't been great at schoolwork. He hadn't had learning difficulties or dyslexia. It was just that he'd had better things to do, like music, tennis and hanging out with friends. Now, Jordan didn't go to school. In a way, school came to him within Unit Red. And his lessons didn't follow any known curriculum.

Jordan's tutor stopped his explanation of the Counter-Terrorism Act in mid-flow and put a hand to the side of his head. After a few seconds of listening to the voice in his earpiece, he said, "That's all for today. Angel wants you in the bunker."

Jordan was pleased to get out of the rest of the day's lessons. He stood by the sliding doors and thought about reaching out with his right arm, extending his forefinger and pushing the centre of the button to call the lift. In an instant, his arm came up and his fingertip touched the button with pinpoint accuracy.

Within a few seconds, the doors opened and he went inside. At once, the cage plunged downwards. He could hear the steel cables slithering over pulleys. He could smell the warm oil that smoothed the motion. The distant scrabbling noise might have been a rat at the bottom of the lift shaft. Jordan turned down both the volume of his hearing and his sense of smell with a couple of thoughts. It had taken months and months of training to master his brain implants. Adjusting the power of his damaged sight, hearing and sense of smell wasn't yet as easy and natural as standing up and walking, but he was now in control of his unique body.

Angel was sitting at his desk, phone on one side, laptop on the other. That was probably all he needed. If someone brought him food and drink, he could probably stay in the bunker for ever.

Standing to his left was a woman Jordan had seen in the house before. With short startling blonde hair and a fantastic figure, she was hard to ignore.

Angel stood up when Jordan came in and, for the first time, offered his right hand.

Jordan looked into his face.

"Yes. Come on. Shake hands," said Angel. "I trust you."

It was a significant moment. There was a time when Jordan would have crushed a real hand completely. He still could if he wanted to. But he had learned to control the strength of his arm using feedback from its pressure-sensitive artificial skin. He thought about it carefully, reached out and clasped Angel's delicate hand with perfect pressure, and then released his grip.

Angel smiled and introduced the woman. "This is Winter."

She stepped forward and also shook his robotic hand without a trace of nervousness. "How you doing?"

"Better than before."

Angel waved him towards a chair. "Sit yourself down. Do you know what day it is?"

Jordan nodded. "It's my birthday, in a way. I was born – sort of – exactly a year ago. New life, new name, new bits and pieces."

Angel chuckled. "You're big for a one-year-old. Very impressive. As I've said before, you're incredibly lucky to be alive. But you've done really well. You put up with all the operations and learned to manage all your enhancements. It hasn't been easy, I know. For one thing, it shows you've got a tremendous thirst for life. That's good."

Jordan was wondering why Angel was giving him a lecture that he'd heard many times before.

"We're entering a new phase," Angel continued. "It's when you pay back the effort and money that's gone into giving you extra time. Let's face it. We've invested very heavily in getting you this far."

Knowing what was coming, Jordan nodded.

"A while ago, you asked me what Unit Red's got to do with you. I imagine you know perfectly well. Have you got your terahertz vision switched on?"

"No."

"To be honest," he said, glancing at Winter, "it's quite unsettling, knowing you can see through our clothes whenever you want to. But why did we give you it? Not because it's every schoolboy's dream, that's for sure. It's so you can spot a concealed weapon at a glance. Your other wavelengths help in all sorts of ways, like seeing in the dark."

"But I'm not a spy."

"You're from a police family. Getting bad people off the streets is in your genes."

"I'm fourteen!"

"Mmm. That's one of the advantages."

"How do you mean?"

"You don't look like an agent." Angel smiled at him. "But you are. It's right there on your ID card. It's a piece of plastic like any ID, but its number makes it exceptional. The first four digits are the same as mine and Winter's – and everyone else's in Unit Red. It's a code known only to us, the secret services and the police. Don't get me wrong. The police don't know anything about us and how we work. They just know they mustn't ask questions when they see that code."

"But..." Jordan took a deep breath. "I think you're mistaking me for some sort of hero."

Angel disagreed. "Not all heroes look like Superman, you know. They come in all shapes and sizes. I reckon I'm pretty good at recognizing them. It's little things – like not giving up when the rest of the world has thrown the towel in." He leaned forward on his desk. "What's the downside? I'll tell you. You can never contact your old friends or relatives. They know Ben Smith's dead." He reached into a drawer, extracted a state-of-the-art mobile phone and handed it to Jordan. "It's yours. I'm sure you won't call anyone you shouldn't." There was an edge to his tone as he stressed the word *sure*. "But what's the upside? A new, powerful life that a lot of people would envy. Winter here will be your handler and backup. She'll provide all the guidance and support you need. You can trust her totally."

Trust, Jordan thought, was earned and not stated as a fact. That was one of his mum's many mottos. He shook his head.

"Don't underestimate the feel-good factor," Angel continued, "of going after bad guys, working for truth and justice."

Jordan could see the point, but he was still wary. "Sounds dangerous."

Angel smiled. "You're equipped to handle it. And we'll fit you with more enhancements as soon as they're developed."

Seeing an opportunity to get what he wanted, Jordan asked, "If I...you know...become an agent, does it mean I can find out who did this to me?"

"Investigate the Thames explosion?"

Jordan nodded.

Angel took a deep breath. "The police never found out who did it. They tried hard, but..." He shrugged. "It's a tough case and you're too emotionally involved. So, the answer's no."

Jordan stood his ground. "My answer's no as well, then."

Angel stared at him for several seconds. "Are you really saying you'll join Unit Red only if I give you the estuary explosion case?"

Surprising himself with his strength of will, he replied, "Yes, I am."

Again, Angel lapsed into silence. Then he sighed. "It's against my better judgement but..."

Jordan's eyes opened wider. "I can go after whoever blew me up?"

Angel nodded reluctantly. "The police investigated it for a year and failed. Now, it's landed in my lap. I've got to delegate it to someone. I didn't want it to be you, but you've forced my hand. So, yes, it's your first mission. At least you've got a good reason to succeed. You'll need more training and plenty of briefings from Winter. You'll have to pass some tough tests. But then you can go out there and catch him."

"Him?"

"I mean him or her. Or them. It could have been a group action."

Jordan realized that Ben Smith had spent too long sitting and learning in school, and not enough time doing things that made an impact. That was because Ben thought he had plenty of time. But Jordan knew that life could be snatched away in a moment. To make the most of his extra time, he had to live fast. He imagined a Unit Red agent would never be short of action. But the most important thing was the desire for truth and justice.

5 GUN

The teams of officers that had worked on the case of the Thames Estuary explosion were not even sure what they'd been investigating. It could have been the work of a crook. It could have been terrorism. It could have been something else, but it probably wasn't an accident. A year after the *Richard Montgomery* blew up, their investigation had stalled. Needing a fresh approach, it was handed over to a boy who died in the massacre and who was reborn as Jordan Stryker.

The novice agent sat quietly in the white Audi as Winter drove at speed towards Medway. No one in Lower Stoke would recognize Jordan when they got there. The passing of a year and the effects of medical reconstruction would take care of that. Jordan hardly recognized himself. He imagined walking up to Amy Goss and watching her face. Zilch. Completely blank. Not a tiny spark of recognition. Besides, she'd believe that he'd died. She might even have gone to his funeral.

Everyone in the affected areas of Kent and Essex had been placed in one of four categories: *Unhurt*, *Injured*, *Deceased*, or *Missing*. Unlike Ben Smith, Amy wasn't listed among the dead. When Jordan had checked, he'd found her name under *Unhurt*. But would he dare to go up to her? Angel had made him promise that he wouldn't get in touch with anyone who knew Ben Smith. Even so, he longed to see Amy and make friends all over again as Jordan Stryker. But he wasn't convinced that he was a good enough actor to pretend he didn't know her. Maybe there would be a giveaway spark of recognition on his face. Anyway, she would have moved on. She would have new friends. Maybe a boyfriend.

Angel had called Jordan special, but he longed to be normal. It wasn't possible. Jordan would never be normal again. He had agreed to become a Unit Red agent and a guinea pig for modern medical technology. His body would be upgraded whenever there were other useful enhancements. And he would use his advanced body and brain to tackle tricky cases and untouchable villains. Starting with the Thames Estuary bomber.

Jordan was determined to unearth the culprit. He wanted to come face-to-face with the person responsible and ask one simple question. *Why?* He needed to know what was worth so much loss of life and his own pain. Then...Jordan wasn't sure. Would handing the bomber over to the police satisfy him? Would he want to go further? In his right arm he had the power to snuff out a life. But could he kill someone he hated? Was his thirst for revenge as strong as his thirst for survival? He didn't know himself well enough. Ben Smith wasn't built like that, but Jordan Stryker was still a mystery. Really, he was a blank slate, waiting for life in Unit Red to define him.

He was sure about one thing, though. He wished that the bomber could go through the same pain and suffering as he had. That appealed to his sense of natural justice.

On cue, Winter said, "I suggest we give the bomber – or bombers – a name. It'll make it easier to talk about him or her...or them." She paused while she thought.

"Red Devil. The *Red* being short for river estuary destroyer. Okay?"

Jordan shrugged. "Okay. Red Devil."

"I won't always be available to drive you around, you know. I'm busy on other things as well. Anyway," she said, dropping down into fourth gear, "I heard you're going to get your own car if things go well."

"A car? But..."

She glanced sideways at him. "You've got false ID. It wouldn't take much to tweak your date of birth so you're old enough. You're big enough to pass for a seventeen-year-old. Just."

Jordan smiled to himself. His own car. Maybe a Ferrari or Porsche. He'd be the only fourteen-year-old on the road. Things weren't all bad.

He looked across at her and said, "Are *you* enhanced in any way?"

"That's an impertinent question to ask a woman!"

"I didn't mean... I just wondered if all agents..."

Winter laughed. "I know what you meant. And, no, I'm all flesh and blood. You're unique – in Unit Red or anywhere else."

As Winter drove, Jordan used his wireless connection to run through the police file on the case. But Amy Goss kept appearing in his mind. Had his imagination conjured up her likeness or had he logged on to a Unit Red file that contained her photo? He wasn't sure, but she was certainly on his mind.

Perhaps she was linked to the case. The local police had looked into the possibility that a rival gang had muscled in on her father's patch and announced itself with a spectacular show of strength. They weren't sure. They knew only that, after the big bang, Mr. Goss was no longer controlling the streets. Some of the same thugs were out there, but they weren't working for Mr. Goss any more. All of the usual police informants were too scared to whisper the name of the new gangland boss and Mr. Goss was keeping a low profile.

Then there was the motive of terrorism. But who or what was the target? Who had come off worst – apart from the Smith family and many other unlucky victims? The police decided that the oil and gas industry had suffered most. That suggested sabotage by an extreme environmental group. Most suspicion fell on an outfit called the Protectors Of Planet Earth – or POPE – headed by Henry Quickfall. Then there was the destruction of Sheerness Animal Breeding Station, possibly by animal rights activists. That was another of Henry Quickfall's activities.

If the police file on possible terrorism had been printed

on paper, it would have filled Winter's car and more. It might have filled a lorry. Jordan hadn't got a hope of absorbing it all. He concentrated on the summaries that Angel had provided.

The Audi lurched as Winter pulled out to overtake. An April shower began to splatter the windscreen, blurring the view. The car detected the moisture and the wipers turned on automatically.

Five protest groups had claimed responsibility for the blast. One was an animal rights outfit, another campaigned against the arms trade, two were radical green movements, and the last was a bunch of political extremists. After examining each claim thoroughly, the police concluded that there was no convincing evidence to back up any of the claims.

Realizing he was out of his depth, Jordan wondered what he had talked himself into. He didn't know what to make of the case. He wasn't an expert. He was just a boy with a strong arm. He'd been taught all about intelligence work by Unit Red, but that didn't make him a professional. Even so, his idea of terrorism didn't match the events of a year earlier.

Surely a terrorist would have rammed a boat at full speed into the wreck of the *Richard Montgomery*, or downed a plane on it, in a spectacular suicide mission.

A fanatic would have gone out in a blaze of glory. Literally. But, according to the police file, Red Devil planted an underwater time bomb or a remote-controlled device on the wreck to provide the opportunity of escape. To Jordan, that seemed too subtle for an act of terrorism. But what did he know about terror campaigns, sabotage and bombs?

One particular lead grabbed Jordan's attention. Red Devil had left the site of the wreck and powered towards Southend-on-Sea, pursued by the river police. That was when the chaos had begun. Before both boats had sunk, the police were able to identify the vessel they were chasing and had radioed its name to their headquarters, but they hadn't got close enough to identify who was in it. When the investigations began, the Quickfall family were immediate suspects because that boat belonged to Henry Quickfall's sister. Cara Quickfall was so closely related to the animal rights and environmental campaigner that the police had questioned her and Henry at length. Both had alibis and denied any knowledge of the explosion. Cara had even reported the theft of her motorboat the day before the bombs went off.

The sinking of Cara Quickfall's boat meant that Red Devil could be lying at the bottom of the river estuary. But almost everyone in the affected area had been accounted for. There was one exception. Jordan caught his breath when he saw it. A schoolteacher called Salam Bool had never been traced after the explosion. After a year, his name was the only one left in the category of *Missing*. If the bomber had died that day, it was either Mr. Bool or an outsider.

Jordan felt nervous as they entered Lower Stoke. He'd promised himself always to look to the future but this assignment was a step back into his past. He reminded himself that it had been his own idea. He'd made the decision to return, and it felt good, after a year of being dependent on others, to be in control of something. Even so, he was uneasy.

He wanted to take a look inside the sports centre because Mr. Goss's heavies used to hang out there. If a new gang had moved into the area, he'd soon see the changes.

Winter wouldn't let him get out at Shepherds Way. That was where Ben Smith used to live and Winter didn't want the residents to see a boy gawping at the houses. Instead, she agreed to drive past slowly. Even so, Jordan's jaw dropped. By the light of the streetlamps, he could see that it was all different. Ben's home had gone.

Totally. Number fourteen and the house next door – number sixteen – were identical new properties. Most of the nearby sheds and garages had vanished. Many had been replaced. Number twelve was a mosaic of the original house and new building. Further along, a terrace of houses with tiny gardens had been squeezed into the space where there had been three roomy homes. Jordan barely recognized the neighbourhood.

Winter stopped the Audi just round the corner from the sports club and turned to Jordan. "Are you sure this is where you want to be?"

He nodded. "Amy's dad owns it. At least, he used to. It was full of kids, but Mr. Goss's people were always there as well. They broke fights up. There's a door in the corner that's always locked. Only Mr. Goss's heavies went in. If someone new's taken over, everything'll be different and I might hear something."

"All right," Winter said. "But remember it's been rebuilt. Part of it anyway."

"Just like me," Jordan replied.

"I showed you the plans."

"Yeah."

"Remember your brief as well," she said. "Avoid confrontation. If it looks like there's going to be trouble, don't get involved. Just leave."

"Sure."

"Tell me the first rule of Unit Red."

"Have you forgotten it?" Jordan said. Because he wasn't really in the mood for joking, he wiped the forced smile from his face and answered properly, "We're always undercover. We never ever mention Unit Red."

Winter nodded, apparently satisfied. "I can't stay here without raising suspicion. I'll be round the corner in the car park."

"Okay."

"And I'll be online." She pointed at the laptop on the back seat. "You can log on any time."

"All right." Jordan got out, closed the door, and took a deep breath of Lower Stoke air. It was surprisingly fresh. The oil refinery and gas terminal had gone. Their tall cylinders were no longer silhouetted against the darkening sky.

At least the rain had stopped. The sports centre's entrance was lit brightly in the evening gloom. As he walked towards it, he remembered how he used to hog the tennis court at the back of the building and, even though he was really young at the time, he'd twice taken the place of a drummer who'd been too ill to perform a gig at the club. Those memories were off limits now. They would only get in the way of what he had to do.

The past is past, as his mum used to say.

He wondered who he would see inside. He would have to play the part of a stranger if he recognized anyone.

Walking past a group of girls drinking cider on the pavement, Jordan didn't linger outside. He had a feeling that, if he hesitated, he might lose his nerve. He opened the door and went straight in. At once, a bouncer had him by the arm. His right arm. Jordan yanked it out of the big man's grasp.

"Hey!" Clearly surprised by Jordan's strength, the bouncer snapped, "What do you think you're doing?"

It hadn't been like this a year earlier. Amy's dad didn't put heavies on the door. "Someone said you've got snooker tables."

"This your first time?"

"Yes," he lied.

"Well, no one gets in without being frisked. Arms and legs out."

The bouncer ran his cupped hands up each leg and said, "What's this bulge?"

Jordan was hardly going to explain the battery implanted under his skin. He pulled up his right trouser leg and replied, "There's nothing. It's swollen, that's all. A medical condition."

The doorman began to feel along both sleeves. Jordan knew that his right arm would not pass for normal. His coat and synthetic skin might disguise its true nature but the flawless fingers would give it away. From a distance they looked real but, close up, they were clearly fake.

"What now?" the bouncer exclaimed.

"A false arm. I lost mine in a car accident."

Unsure, the doorman grimaced. "Well..."

"You're not going to stop me because I'm disabled, are you?" Jordan hated that word. He wasn't disabled. He was more than able. He was enhanced. But he was willing to exploit the word when it worked in his favour.

"Can you play snooker with it?"

He nodded.

The bouncer eyed him suspiciously and then carried on with the search. His hands patted Jordan's back and chest. Then he stepped away. "Okay. You're in. But no funny business."

The sports hall looked different. Less busy, but still well used. The snooker and pool tables were on the left. Beyond them was the entrance to the gym, climbing wall and boxing ring. Table tennis and a suite of computer games were on the right. The dartboards at the back were unused. The door at the far end was still there and so was a sleazy group of people in their twenties and thirties.

And the racket! Maybe it had always been noisy and he'd never really noticed. Now, with fantastic hearing, it was like being surrounded by chanting football fans. Yet Jordan didn't want to turn down the volume. He was trying to pick out any conversation that might tell him if this bit of Mr. Goss's territory was under new management – and, if so, who was in charge. Instinct told him to get as close as possible to the group at the far end. They were just hanging around, not playing games, in the area that Mr. Goss's heavies used to occupy.

Strolling down the aisle between the various games, he spotted only a few faces that were familiar. Two boys playing pool used to be in one of Ben Smith's classes. He recognized three younger girls chatting near the computer games, but he didn't know their names. A lot of the people were beyond school age and new to him. The sports centre was attracting a different crowd altogether.

Lingering near the final snooker table, Jordan soon realized what the men by the door were doing. Watching them and catching snatches of whispered exchanges told him that they were dealing drugs. Jordan was shocked. Mr. Goss wouldn't have allowed it. Amy's dad wasn't exactly on the same wavelength as the law but, as far as Jordan knew, he didn't do deals with children. His heavies would have moved in on anyone trying to take advantage of the local kids. After all, he had a daughter to protect from that sort of thing.

"Oi!" one of the dealers shouted. "What are you doing?"

Jordan was nearly deafened. "Nothing."

Two of them came over to him. "That's what they all say. At first. What are you after?"

"I'm looking for a friend," Jordan replied. "Nothing else."

The two men laughed. One yelled over his shoulder, "He's just looking for a friend!"

"Haven't heard that before. Bring him over here."

Jordan felt a hollowness in his stomach as the dealers pushed him in the back and the pack parted to let him through. Before he'd worked out what to do, he had his back to the door and a threatening mob in his face. He wasn't certain but two of the young men might once have been Mr. Goss's heavies.

The ringleader said, "You come to buy or you keep clear. If you come to spy..." He shrugged theatrically. "What are we supposed to make of that? We might think you had something to do with the law. That wouldn't be good for your health. Know what I mean?" The man's mouth was a black hole within a circle of bushy beard but the top of his head was completely bald.

Jordan's terahertz vision told him that, underneath the man's sweatshirt, he had a gun tucked into his trouser belt.

After all he'd been through, Jordan thought he'd outlived the fear of being hurt. But he was still scared. He could feel sweat running down between his shoulder blades like a cold glass marble. "Kids my age don't become cops," he said.

"You don't look like a customer either. So, I ask myself, what are you?"

"I haven't been here before. I didn't know what was going on so I came to check it out. That's all."

The dealer interrupted. "Do I look like someone who believes in fairy stories?"

No. He looked like a thug. "I didn't mean to..."

"You said you were looking for a friend. Changed your mind?"

Jordan shrugged.

"You're on your own. What are we?" The big guy looked from side to side. "Eight? Ten? All used to taking care of business. Know what I mean? You're cornered. Up against a locked door. No way out."

Jordan should have been able to open a link to Winter's laptop with his brain/computer interface and ask for backup. With these guys in his face, though, he couldn't summon up the necessary concentration. Anyway, he hated the idea of admitting he needed help within minutes of his first job.

He knew he should have taken Winter's advice already to get out before trouble started. He hoped he wasn't too late. He took a deep breath, twisted and stabbed his false fist at the door. The wood was too thick to splinter but the lock could not withstand the force of his punch. It shattered and the door swung inwards.

Jordan dashed inside while the men stood and stared in amazement. He knew he only had a moment before the heavies on the other side of the door reacted. He scanned the room. Large grey filing cabinets, a huge desk, a safe and a fire exit to the right. On the left, there was some sort of laboratory bench. His amplified sense of smell detected something vaguely chemical.

He turned towards the only exit but didn't dare to move towards it. The guy with the gun had stepped into the room. He wasn't hiding the weapon any more. He was pointing it at Jordan's chest.

Jordan stopped and put his hands up.

"You're not in a cowboy film," the man said with a

cruel grin. "You're in deep trouble." The smirk was replaced by an expression of sheer malice. "No one comes in here. And no one messes with us like that. No one. The boss'll want to meet you."

It wasn't an invitation. It was a demand.

"Who's that?" Jordan asked. Trying to keep his voice under control, he lowered his arms.

"Come with me."

It was an opportunity to find out who had taken over the club from Mr. Goss, Jordan realized, but it was too risky. It would be pointless to discover the godfather's identity but not get out alive. If these people had blown up half of Medway, they wouldn't hesitate to dispose of one fourteen-year-old boy. After all, he didn't officially exist and they might have killed him once already. "I don't think so," he replied.

"I'll end it here and now, then." The thug took aim.

6 HURT

Jordan didn't know what he'd said, seen or done to provoke such an extreme reaction. Facing execution, his legs were quaking. But he remained alert. His eyes picked out the first movement of the man's forefinger on the trigger. Jordan thought of his bionic arm protecting his heart. Immediately, his arm moved in front of his chest and the bullet clanged against his hand. The force of the blow knocked his forearm harmlessly into his body and the bullet bounced away. There was no blood, no wound.

The gangster's mouth and eyes opened wide. He took at least five seconds to respond. "Who are you?" Astonished, he added, "*What* are you?"

Jordan was stunned as well. His tense fingers locked onto the desktop and his right hand began to crush the wood. "Just a boy," he said, pretending to be calm as the adrenalin surged around his body. Then he lifted the entire desk and threw it at the startled bunch of dealers. He didn't wait to see it hit home. He didn't wait for the havoc it would cause. As he made for the fire exit at full speed, he heard the crash, the cries and swearing behind him. His right arm hit the door first and it burst open. He dashed round the tennis court and onto the club's football pitch.

He didn't hesitate in case any of the men had recovered from the shock and were about to chase him. Wishing he had bionic legs as well, he doubled back. He didn't turn right to return to the crossroads where Winter would be waiting in the car park, because the streetlamps along the straight road would keep him in view for several minutes. Instead, he went to the left and, after a few metres, right into Button Drive. Grateful for the darkness, he was out of sight of the club within seconds. Besides, no one would expect him to go in that direction. Almost everyone thought of it as a no-through-road, but not Jordan. He hurried to the end and sprinted round the back of the flats. He scrambled over the wooden fence and hurtled across the narrow field towards the farmyard and its grain silos.

Jordan didn't try to count the metal containers but there seemed to be fewer than he remembered. Panting, he came to a halt between three of the silos, hidden from the world, and sank onto the damp ground. It was only after he'd got his breath back that he blinked and scanned the blackened gap with infrared vision. He let out a gasp. Two paces away, there was a yellow and red glow in the shape of a human figure crouching in the darkness.

"Hello?" Jordan called. "Is someone there?" Of course, he knew that someone was lurking in his secret hideout.

A familiar voice called out, "Who are you?"

Amy! Jordan hoped that she didn't hear him gasp again. At least the darkness hid the emotions on his face. She was a gleaming warmth to him but he'd be a bare outline to her. "Jordan," he said.

"Sounds like you've been running."

Straight away, he recognized an opportunity. "I...er... got into trouble with the guys in the sports centre."

Amy's voice became urgent and edgy. "They aren't following you, are they?"

"No. Do you know them?"

"I used to know the people who ran it, but not this lot."

The glimmer was not exactly Amy-shaped. She was taller now. But it was definitely Amy plus a year. Talking to her, Jordan's heart was hammering as much as it had when he'd confronted the dealers, but for an entirely different reason. "They didn't seem very nice."

"No."

He wanted to rush over to her, give her a hug and whisper, "It's me. I'm back." But that was one thing he could never do. In his enthusiasm, he might even have hurt her. He tried to focus on what he was supposed to be doing. Those drug dealers were clearly operating with the full knowledge of the new owner. "Who are they?" he said. "Who runs it now?"

She didn't answer right away. Perhaps she was suspicious. Perhaps she thought he was asking too many questions. "Do you know what's weird?"

"What?"

"You haven't asked me why I'm here."

"Why are you?"

Amy paused. "Because I meet my friend here."

So, she had a new friend. Or she was trying to give the impression that someone could turn up at any second because she felt threatened. "When's he coming?"

"Who said it was a he?"

"I just...assumed."

"Another thing that's weird. You told me your name but you didn't ask me mine."

"I was scared you might think I was...you know."

"Chatting me up?" Amy laughed softly. "You can't even see me."

"No."

"Your voice is a bit strange. You speak like a local but you don't go to our school."

"Home tuition," Jordan replied. He knew that today was the first day of the summer term but it made no difference to him.

"So you go to the club because you don't do sport at school."

Jordan nodded but, remembering that she couldn't see him, he said, "Yes."

"Bad mistake," Amy muttered. Then she added, "I don't like the people in charge – to put it mildly – and they don't like you. I suppose that puts you and me on the same side."

"I guess."

Amy drew in a deep breath. "Everyone around here's too frightened to talk..." She went quiet for a few seconds. "The new Mr. Big isn't Mr. Big at all. It's Ms. Big, I suppose. My dad says it's someone called Melissa Pink."

"A woman. When did she take over?"

"Straight after the river blast. A year ago. He said she's not from round here."

At once, Jordan's brain fumbled around for the right thoughts that would log him on to Unit Red's system. *Melissa Pink. Criminal activity.*

When he established a link, the visual effect was like looking at a shop window. He would see the display inside and, at the same time, a reflection of what was behind him. Right now, Amy's shape shone through the scrolling pages of Melissa Pink's file.

It seemed that Pink was the mastermind behind the Midlands crime scene. She'd never been convicted of a serious crime, but the police were in no doubt that she was responsible for much of it. They also regarded her as ruthless and vicious. Even so, Jordan did not spot any references to bombings in her record. If she'd moved in on Kent with a devastating explosion, she'd also stepped up several leagues in violence.

"You've gone quiet," Amy said. "Have you heard of Pink?"

"No," he answered.

"She's vile, according to Dad. Way beyond cruel." Looking like a candle flame that had suddenly elongated, Amy got to her feet. "I'm off," she announced abruptly as she walked away. She'd done it so often in the dark that she didn't bump into the sides of the silos.

Jordan called after her, "If I see your friend, I'll tell him you've gone."

For a moment, the flame flared yellow. "I don't think you'll see him. It's too late."

Abandoned, Jordan watched her stroll down the track. When her radiance faded to nothing, he experienced a twinge around his stomach. One of his wounds there hadn't healed properly. The hurt had never really gone away and he was left with a sensitive scar. That's how he felt over Amy as well.

In the Gillingham safe house, Winter gazed at him like a mother who had just heard a pack of lies from her son. "So, it all went smoothly. You didn't bump into anyone you recognized, you saw drug dealers who weren't there before the big bang, and you heard them saying a woman called Melissa Pink is in charge?"

Jordan nodded. "That's it." He was determined to keep quiet about meeting Amy.

"Took a long time."

Jordan shrugged. "They talked about a lot of other stuff first."

"Such as?"

"Football." Trying to avoid further interrogation, Jordan said, "What I don't know is whether Melissa Pink planted the estuary bomb or just took advantage of it. Maybe she made her move on Mr. Goss's business when everyone was...you know..."

"Panicking?"

"Yeah."

"And while you were listening to the football chat, you smelled a chemical sort of smell."

"Like, from a lab."

"But you don't know what it was?"

"No."

To Jordan, Winter didn't look like a mother. She looked stunning, even though she was about thirty. An occasional peek with terahertz vision was impossible to resist.

She'd taught him the Unit Red rules, but Jordan preferred his mum's nuggets of advice on life. His mum had been full of them. She never went on, though. Her advice came in pithy one-liners, like proverbs. Often, they were serious. Sometimes, they weren't. Her advice on women? "When you're living in a house with the opposite sex, don't leave the toilet seat up." Jordan's inward smile was sad and wry.

Winter gulped back some coffee. "I think our chemist ought to take you through a few smells in case you can pin it down. Starting with the whiff of a bomb-making factory. And we need to know a lot more about what Melissa Pink's up to. Then there's the disciplinary action against you."

"What?"

She smiled and pointed to his right hand. "Damaging government property."

Jordan glanced down at the patch of artificial skin that the bullet had ripped out. "Ah, that."

She nodded. "How did it happen?"

He didn't want to admit to his handler that, on his very first outing as a Unit Red agent, he hadn't obeyed her instruction to keep out of trouble. "I...er...caught it on the door. I'm still a bit...you know."

"Economical with the truth?"

"No. Clumsy."

Winter shook her head, laughed and swigged the rest of her coffee. "The technician who'll repair it will work out what caused it and tell us, even if you won't."

"Changing the subject..." he said.

Winter's mug was decorated with two cartoon frogs. She put it down and gazed at him.

"I think you should trace Salam Bool's mobile. It went missing the same day as the explosion."

Winter was taken aback. "How do you know?"

"He was one of my...I mean, one of Ben Smith's teachers. And he was in a temper because someone had nicked it."

"I'll get onto it. I want to figure out if we can get you close to Melissa Pink as well, but it'd be pushing you in at the deep end. Especially now her people have seen you. So, let's try something else first. A shallow-end tactic."

"Like what?"

"I think you should make friends with the Quickfall kids. See if you can find out anything about the family's animal rights and environmental activities. The question is, would they go as far as bombing? Are they that radical?" She stood up. "That's after a visit to the lab to get your hand fixed – and before you forget that smell."

7 KNIFE

The train ran alongside the river estuary on its approach to Southend Central. The wrecks of *Ocean Courage* and the oil supertanker were no longer cluttering the waterway. They had been salvaged and removed to clear the important shipping lane.

Just before the train rattled through Chalkwell Station, it passed some small boatyards on the right. Jordan watched out for them because Cara Quickfall had kept her boat there until it went missing. Straight after the station, on the left, were the tennis courts where Cara's sons went after school every Tuesday and Thursday.

Jordan looked down at his robotic arm. His attitude to it had changed. Had it been only flesh and blood, he would not have got out of the sports club alive. The mechanical hand was perfect again. The technician had diagnosed the damage straight away. "Someone's hammered a pointed tool against it or you've been shot." The patches on Jordan's face that were natural skin had turned bright red. Without mentioning Amy, he'd admitted what had happened. No doubt the story would make its way to Angel and Winter so he expected a telling-off soon.

Back in the Unit Red labs, he'd been taken to the chief chemist. She'd listened to him and then said, "You probably got a whiff of a volatile solvent." She'd taken him to a fume cupboard and asked him to sniff a series of liquids. The first one to catch his attention had been acetone. "It's not quite right," he'd told her, "but it was something like that." She'd thought about it for a few seconds, mixed two solvents together and told him to try again. And that was it. Exactly. She'd nodded. "You said they were dealing drugs. That was the clue. It's not about bomb-making. A one-to-one mix of diethyl ether and acetone is the classic solvent for purifying cocaine. It's more than likely you stumbled across an illicit drug lab."

That was probably why Melissa Pink's henchmen had turned so nasty. He'd seen the laboratory and they were not going to let him leave with that knowledge.

"Shouldn't we send the police in?" Jordan had asked.

"I'll mention it to Angel, but I know what he'll say. It's too late. They'll have moved the operation as soon as you compromised it. Drug factories appear and disappear all the time. Otherwise, they'd get caught."

The train jerked and Jordan swayed in his seat. He looked at the girl sitting opposite him. She almost returned his smile but carried on reading her magazine. She had no idea that he could listen to every conversation in the coach, detect passengers with bad breath, and see straight through everyone's clothes if he turned on his terahertz vision with a single thought. He wouldn't try it all at once, though, because he would be overwhelmed, like a website crashed by information overload.

The train arrived only two minutes late. Jordan had time to stroll along the esplanade on his way to the tennis club.

The front had been battered by the force of the estuary blast and, in places, it was still being mended. The long pier had been mangled but emergency repairs had made it serviceable. One of the boathouses remained out of action and a nearby block of flats was covered with scaffolding. The riverside gardens had mostly recovered. They were lined with benches in memory of people who'd died in the explosion. Jordan stopped to gaze sadly on the memorials for a few seconds. So many benches squeezed together. There were more benches than people on the front to sit on them.

Jordan had learned the route to the tennis club but, if he got lost, he could go online and consult a map in his mind. He checked the time. It was very important for him to be precisely on schedule. Turning his back on the seafront, he went along Chalkwell Avenue, under the railway bridge, and up to the club. He arrived at the same time as two rough men who, judging by their physique, spent a lot of time in a gym. He stood aside to let them in first.

Jordan had also memorized pictures of Cara Quickfall's sons. They were twelve and thirteen years old, white and fair-haired. Their upmarket clothes suggested that they weren't short of cash. He found them in the changing rooms. But the two beefy guys had found them first.

The brothers were pinned against a row of lockers and one of the muggers was shouting, "Come on! Mobiles, cash and iPods. Now!"

Turning on his terahertz vision, Jordan saw that the man who was shouting had a knife in his trouser pocket.

"Oi!" Jordan said. "Leave them alone."

"Stay out of it, you."

Jordan refused. "Pick on someone your own size."

Angered by his intervention, both men turned and came threateningly towards him. "You're closer to our size." The first thug delved into his pocket, extracted the knife and thrust it in Jordan's direction.

Jordan dropped his sports bag. His right arm shot out and snatched the knife before the mugger could react. Jordan wrapped his fingers around the blade and bent it back on itself as easily as folding paper. He handed the buckled knife back to its owner without a word.

The man stared at the useless thing in his palm. "How did you...?" Instead of finishing his question, he turned tail and ran away, along with his mate.

The Quickfall boys stood and stared at Jordan. Then the younger one cried, "That was awesome!"

"Thanks," his brother said.

Jordan shrugged. "No problem."

It really wasn't a problem. The men were Unit Red agents and they'd staged the attack. They'd expected Jordan to step in and save the boys. The whole set-up was Winter's idea to give Jordan a way of befriending the Quickfall brothers.

"Look, er..." The older boy hesitated. "What's your name?"

"Jordan."

"I'm Brady and he's Reece. I don't fancy staying here. Not after that."

Reece hesitated. "We can't go! What if they're waiting for us outside?"

"I'll come with you, if you like," Jordan said. "They won't take on three of us."

"Not after what you just did." Brady shook his head in disbelief. "Is your hand okay?"

Jordan held it out. "Fine."

"Hey. What is that?" Brady prodded it with his forefinger.

Jordan stuck to the explanation he'd agreed with Angel to avoid awkward questions. "It's false. A car crash got rid of my real one."

"Cool!" said Reece. "Is that how come you can bend metal – because you're bionic?"

"I'm not bionic," Jordan lied, "but a false arm has its uses."

Reece seemed fascinated. "Can you take it off?"

"Not really. I don't wear it like a shoe or anything. It's

attached." He could easily remove individual fingers or the hand, but not the whole arm. To do that, he'd need the help of a Unit Red engineer.

"You'd make a neat bodyguard," Brady said with a grin.

"Yeah. You already saved us," Reece added.

"I bet Mum'd like to thank you," Brady said. "Do you want to come back to our place?"

Jordan hesitated. He didn't want to appear too eager.

"Go on," said Reece. "We've got some pretty hot computer games."

"Well, they've got to be better for you than tennis," Jordan replied.

"How come?"

"You don't get beaten up while you're getting ready."

For a moment, Brady looked puzzled. "How did you know we were going to play tennis?"

Jordan felt a jolt inside as he realized his mistake. Trying not to show it, he shrugged. "It's a tennis club."

"That's not all. There's a gym and a pool."

Reece groaned at his suddenly suspicious brother.

Jordan decided to take a risk. "I saw a tennis racket in your locker, didn't I?"

"Oh, yeah," said Brady. "A bit of a giveaway. What are you doing here?"

"How do you mean?"

"Were you going to play tennis as well?"

Reece butted in. "You'd be great."

Jordan shook his head. "I could probably serve faster than anyone else on the planet and put enough spin on the ball to win every point. But one of the rules says, 'Every player must hold the racket with a real arm.'"

Giggling, Reece replied, "It'd be fun, though."

Jordan nodded. "Sure would."

"So, what are you here for?" Brady asked.

"The pool," Jordan told him, picking up his bag. "I was going swimming."

"Do you go rusty?" said Reece.

Jordan laughed. "I shower every day and it hasn't happened yet. Swimming's supposed to be good for my muscles."

Satisfied at last, Brady nodded.

Reece sighed with relief. "Are you coming home with us, then?"

Jordan pretended to think about it. He wasn't proud of tricking the Quickfall boys, but he was on a mission. That was his excuse for being devious. He glanced at his watch and then said, "All right. But..."

"What?"

"I'm not sure I'll be any good at computer games. Because of this." He waved his artificial arm.

The Quickfalls' energy-efficient house looked a bit like Unit Red's headquarters, without the gravestones and secret network of underground rooms. The front was largely glass and odd angles. The roof was a mass of solar panels and the gutters fed rainfall into a large tank. Standing inside, Jordan could hear the quiet rumble of a pump. It was bringing up water from pipes buried deep in the garden, using the natural warmth of the earth to heat the house.

Jordan listened to Reece's booming voice whilst trying to eavesdrop on the whispered conversation between Brady and his mother in the next room.

"Did it hurt?" Reece asked. "I mean, when your arm got ripped off."

"But who is he?" Cara's hushed voice said in the background. "You've got to be careful after what happened."

"No," Jordan answered. "I was unconscious, I suppose. More than that. My heart stopped beating so I guess I was sort of dead. Didn't feel a thing."

"You died?"

Meanwhile, Brady was whispering to his mum, "I know, but he's okay. He saved us."

"Saved you?"

Brady began to tell his mum about the incident with the knife while Jordan replied to Reece, "They resuscitated me. That's when it hurt. When I came round it was agony. They gave me bucketfuls of painkillers."

Realizing that Jordan was distracted, Reece said, "It's only mum checking up on you." He shook his head and sighed. "She gets in a state about who we mix with."

Just a mother taking care of her sons, Jordan thought. If only he still had a mother... But there was no point in feeling sorry for himself. He had Angel, Winter and a whole gang of Unit Red technicians to take care of him. Yet somehow, they didn't make up for his parents. In a way, he still felt alone.

Like any normal family, the Quickfalls probably wanted to murder each other half of the time, but they would always support each other in adversity. Jordan had neither the frustrations nor the safety net of a family now.

Reece was setting up some games when Brady and his mum came in. Cara Quickfall had short dark hair and a pair of glasses resting on top of her head. Jordan wondered if her hairstyle had been designed to keep her spectacles stable. Balanced there, they served no obvious purpose. They were more fashion statement than visual aid. She looked at the visitor and said, "Hi. Brady's been telling me what you did. I appreciate it. Very much. What did you say your surname was?"

"Stryker. Jordan Stryker."

She nodded. "Where do you live?"

"London."

"Oh. What are you doing here?"

"My folks have come for the day. They're into boats. They let me go to the sports club instead." He checked his watch. "I'll have to go and meet them in an hour."

"We used to have a boat," Reece said.

Cara Quickfall cast a warning glance at her son. "Reece..." When she looked back at Jordan, the stern expression had gone. "What about school?" she asked.

"I don't go."

Reece interrupted. "Lucky you."

"I get home tuition."

Brady stared at his mum. "Interrogation over yet?"

Cara smiled. "Just one more question. Can I get you a drink? And something to eat? Any of you?"

She didn't have fizzy drinks, only fruit juice that tasted far too healthy. She didn't have crisps, only wholesome biscuits that tasted of nothing. But Jordan was getting what he needed most: the friendship and trust of the Quickfall kids. Despite his best efforts, though, he could not think his way into the family's computer.

He looked at Reece and said quietly, "Your mum didn't want you talking about the boat you had. What's that all about?"

The two brothers eyed each other before Brady replied, "Sore point."

Reece took up the story. "You know the explosion a year ago?"

Jordan nodded. "It was all over the internet and telly."

"Well, whoever did it nicked our boat. That's how they got out to the wreck."

Jordan did his best to look surprised. "No. Really?"

Reece nodded. "She won't get another one. Says it's too dangerous."

"As if it could happen again," Brady muttered.

"Hey," Jordan said, "does that mean you were all suspects?"

They nodded.

"I bet the police were all over you."

"Mum and Uncle Henry."

"Amazing." Lowering his voice, Jordan said, "Do you think they had anything to do with it?"

"Not Mum," Brady replied at once. Acting as if he needed to supply proof, he added, "She didn't go out that night."

"But Uncle Henry..." Reece shrugged.

"You shouldn't say that, Reece."

"It's true. Uncle Henry's into all sorts of stuff."

"Yeah," Brady replied. "Protests and that sort of thing, but not killing people. No way!"

In the background, Jordan heard footsteps leading to the door but no one came in. He assumed that Cara was lingering out of sight so that she could listen in secret. "What's he got to protest about?"

"Airport runways, motorways, burning oil and coal..."

Reece butted in, "And animals."

"Animals?" said Jordan. "What have they done?"

"No," Brady replied. "Cruelty to animals. You know. Experimenting on them, eating them, and wearing fur. He got done for smashing up the Animal Breeding Station in Sheerness."

"And for attacking the oil terminal," Reece added. "And..."

"But he's nice," Brady said. "Not a mad bomber."

"I think your uncle's right," Jordan replied. "Ages ago, I got cautioned at a demo."

"Why? What for?"

"Damaging a road-building machine. It was going to rip up our playing fields. Just to make a road wider."

"You should meet Uncle Henry," said Brady.

Jordan suspected that talking to him would be a waste of time. If Henry Quickfall was Red Devil, he'd lied successfully to the police. If Jordan spoke to him, he'd lie again. Jordan would prefer to listen in on a conversation between Henry and someone he trusted. Then he would tell the truth.

Jordan remembered from Henry Quickfall's file that the authorities had tapped his telephone calls. He guessed that Unit Red could do it again. Trying to focus on two things at the same time, Jordan logged on to Unit Red's computer and thought a message into the system. *Get ready to record a telephone exchange between Cara and Henry Quickfall.* Then, knowing that Cara was eavesdropping behind the door, he continued to provide her with a reason to call her brother. "He sounds pretty interesting," said Jordan.

"For an uncle," Reece replied, "he's cool."

"Has he got his own boat?"

"No. He used ours."

"Oh dear."

Reece frowned. "What do you mean?"

Jordan explained, "Using the bomber's boat puts him in the frame for being the bomber."

"Sounds like you know about these things," Brady said.

"My mum's in the police." With that, Jordan thought he'd done enough. As long as Cara had overheard, she would surely want to tell Henry. "Hey!" Jordan said, pointing at the monitor. "You beat me. I wasn't concentrating."

Reece laughed. "Lame excuse. It's just that I'm better."

Happy to let him win, Jordan put down the controller. "I'll give you that."

8 ELIMINATED

The vessels moored in Chalkwell Marina varied from expensive yachts to small scruffy motorboats that were taking on water. Any of them would be easy to steal, Jordan realized as he walked slowly along the wooden platform, checking out each one.

Before long, a man chased after Jordan. As solid as a rugby player, he had a short and precisely sculptured beard. He also had the whiff of cigars and alcohol about him. "Can I help you, young man?" he called out.

"Are you in charge?" Jordan asked.

"Yes."

Jordan had already decided what to say. "Oh, good. Have you got any part-time jobs? You know. After school and weekends."

The boatyard manager looked him up and down with a curious expression. "Why would you want to work here? No one else does."

"Why not?"

"Ever since the explosion." He inclined his head towards the estuary. "They think it's not safe. But now the *Richard Montgomery*'s gone, it can't happen again."

Jordan nodded. "The boat came from here, didn't it?"

"Which boat?"

"The one the terrorist used."

The manager seemed suspicious that a teenager should bring up the subject. He asked, "Who are you?"

"Jordan Stryker. I live up the road." He paused before adding, "And I'm short of cash."

"Ah. A job. Yes. Well..." He stroked his neatly trimmed beard. "What do you know about boats?"

"I'm a quick learner."

"Mmm. Nothing, then. I could use some help with

admin, though. How are you on maths, organization and computers?"

Jordan smiled. "The best."

"Would your teachers agree with that? Can you get them to send me a reference?"

Jordan imagined that Angel would write a glowing recommendation if he needed it. "No problem. I'll get it e-mailed. What's your address?"

The man took a business card from the breast pocket of his jacket and handed it over. Jordan glanced at it and said, "Norman Lightfoot."

With a smile, Norman said, "At least that proves you can read."

"If you show me your computer, I'll prove I'm good with that as well."

Norman hesitated for a while and then replied, "Why not? A quick test. Come this way." He walked stiffly, shoulders back like an army officer, to the shack at the edge of the marina. His manner was more pompous than Jordan would have expected for a boatyard manager.

Inside, the walls were plastered with pictures of boats and ships, and the air carried the smell of whisky and cigar smoke. The main room had several filing cabinets, a couple of chairs, a desk and a computer. On the monitor was a spreadsheet. Each entry named a boat and its owner, a mooring reference, payment details, and other particulars.

"Yes," Jordan said at once, "I know this program. I've used it before." Taking hold of the mouse, he scrolled down the document. There was only one owner under the letter Q. "Look. The Quickfall boat. I know Cara Quickfall. Her sons are mates of mine." He peered at the monitor a little too eagerly. "The boat was last used a year ago. By Cara's brother, just before..."

Norman leaned across him and logged out of the program. "You don't want a job, do you? You're just... prying. I don't know what your game is, but I want you to leave."

Jordan shrugged as if he didn't understand Mr. Lightfoot's uneasiness. "Okay. But I was just showing you I could operate the system – using a family I know."

The manager stood beside the computer protectively and kept his eye on Jordan until he was out of the door.

Jordan hadn't learned much from the marina. He imagined that experienced Unit Red agents developed clever plans that took them straight to the answer. He imagined them wrapping up their missions quickly and efficiently. He imagined they'd never be shouldered off the ball as easily as Norman Lightfoot had just done to him.

* * *

Fun was returning to Southend's funfair. Not all of the rides had been replaced or repaired but people had begun to enjoy the fairground again. With his back to the park, Jordan leaned on the rail and looked out at the wounded pier and the wide estuary. He turned down his hearing because the mechanical noises, excited cries and terrified screams coming from the rides threatened to overwhelm him.

Jordan was online, thinking his way around Unit Red's documents with Angel instructing him via mobile phone. "Yes," Angel said. "Open the one called *Quickfall 17/04/2012*. It's a transcript of the Quickfalls' telephone conversation." He hesitated before adding, "I'll give you a minute to read it."

Using the brain/computer interface in his head, Jordan found it easier to read with his eyes closed.

Cara Quickfall: Hi. It's me.
Henry Quickfall: How's it going?
C.Q.: Maybe it's nothing but the boys have just made a new friend. Jordan Stryker. Son of a police officer. Reece talked a bit too much – like always – and mentioned you and the boat. That

set this lad off. He was asking all about you.

H.Q.: Oh? How old is he?

C.Q.: A teenager. Sixteen, maybe. A bit funny-looking. With a false arm.

H.Q.: The police aren't going to recruit their kids, Cara.

C.Q.: But...I don't know. He was fishing for information.

H.Q.: It's over, Cara. The police tried, failed, and gave up. They're not going to catch whoever did it now. And this funny-looking kid... What was his name again?

C.Q.: Jordan Stryker.

H.Q.: Yeah. Stryker. He sounds normal to me, fascinated by bombs and bodies. I was at that age.

C.Q.: Maybe I'm too jittery, but...

H.Q.: What?

C.Q.: I just don't want the whole thing kicking off again.

H.Q.: I don't see why it should, just because a kid's asked a few questions. Even if it does, we've got nothing to worry about. It may have been your boat but it wasn't your fault, and I'm not mad enough to let bombs off. I don't know any

*activists who are, apart from Max and we both
know what happened to him.*

C.Q.: Okay. [Silence for 2 seconds.] *Look, I'll see
you on Sunday. All right?*

H.Q.: Sure. Take care. And don't worry. [Call
ends.]

"Nice work," Angel said.

"Really?"

"You've probably eliminated two suspects. It was Cara
Quickfall's boat but not her fault, and Henry Quickfall
isn't mad enough. Unless he's keeping it from his sister
– which I doubt."

"Who's Max?"

"Ah. Mad Max," Angel replied. "I checked police files.
He's an animal rights campaigner and he's not a suspect.
The night the *Richard Montgomery* went up, he'd broken
into Sheerness Animal Breeding Station with a firebomb.
That's irony for you. He was freeing the animals when
the building collapsed and killed him."

"What now?" Jordan asked.

"Get on a train back to Kent. I'm intrigued by the
missing science teacher, Salam Bool. He bought a new
mobile after school on the day of the explosion. I've
checked phone records. He called his previous number

over and over again that evening from a few locations near Strood."

"So," Jordan guessed, "he went around phoning his old mobile, hoping he'd hear it ring. Then he could get it back."

"That would be my interpretation as well. But how did he know where to go? I think it must have had GPS Tracker technology, so he knew which postcode it was in."

"There must have been something really important on it," said Jordan, almost to himself. Then he added, "And whoever nicked it didn't turn it off. It must have been ringing. Mr. Bool wouldn't wander around calling it if the phone was dead. There wouldn't be any point."

"Absolutely," Angel replied. "Which almost certainly rules out organized crime. A gang dealing in black-market phones would whip the SIM card out and replace it in no time."

"What happens if you ring it now?"

"Nothing. It's out of commission."

"Shame. But why would anyone pinch his phone and leave it on for hours?" Jordan asked.

"Over to you. But it's interesting to speculate what would have happened if he'd come face-to-face with whoever took it."

"So, do you know where he was when he made the last call with his new phone?"

Angel laughed. "Thought you'd never ask. Network operators can track the location of mobiles these days. He was at Hoo Marina."

"I know it. Some of the kids from school hung out there. On the headland."

"Look into it," Angel said. "And Jordan..."

"What?"

"Don't get yourself shot this time."

9 CAUSTIC

Jordan had tricked his way into the Quickfall family, but the same sly tactic was useless for Mr. Bool. The police had not traced any living relatives. They discovered only that he had been engaged years earlier, but his fiancée had run off with another man. The rejection seemed to have hit him hard because, from that point, he'd sunk into an addiction to gambling. He owed a lot of money to a seedy loan company called *EasyCash OnLine*. Really, it was more a one-man loan shark than a company.

The police had no evidence that *EasyCash OnLine* was behind Mr. Bool's disappearance, even though other clients who got into arrears with their payments sometimes ended up in hospital casualty wards.

The official investigation of Salam Bool had not got much further than that. In the days that followed the disaster, when the police combed the missing man's house, forensic specialists examined the hard disk of his home computer. They found that Mr. Bool had used thorough disk deletion software. None of his documents and programs remained.

This was a man who wanted to remain a mystery, or who had planned to disappear, Jordan reckoned. A man with secrets to keep hidden. A man anxious about the information on his computer. Jordan also knew that he'd been anxious about the information on his missing mobile. The police report made no mention of it. Clearly, the investigators hadn't known about the stolen phone.

The police had turned up only one tasty fact. There was a short message on his landline phone. It had been recorded a few minutes after the *Richard Montgomery* explosion. An unidentified male voice on a withheld number said simply, "I hear you've done the job. I'll be in touch." Immediately suspicious, the police had doubled the number of officers assigned to the search for Mr. Bool, but without success.

Jordan had three possible starting points: Mr. Bool's empty house, his last known whereabouts in Hoo, and the kids who were his students at the time of his disappearance. Like Amy.

Jordan wasn't convinced that breaking into Mr. Bool's deserted house would help. He didn't know what he could do there that the police hadn't already done. So he decided to use one advantage he had over the police. His youth. He could mix with the school kids at Hoo Marina. If the police attempted to talk to them, they'd scatter and the ones who didn't scatter quickly enough would clam up. Getting them to talk about Mr. Bool was Jordan's plan. Where it would take him, he didn't know. But he was willing to try anything to unmask Red Devil.

He wanted to look around the marina before they arrived so he went during school time. And that was a mistake. Near the entrance, a uniformed policeman shouted at him. "Hey, you! Stop!"

The officer strolled towards Jordan deliberately slowly, presumably to give him plenty of time to get nervous.

"What's your name?" the policeman asked.

"Jordan Stryker."

"How old are you?"

Jordan was about to answer truthfully, but changed his mind. "Seventeen."

The officer smirked at him. "Why the hesitation?"

"Did I?"

"You could be seventeen, but I'm guessing younger. And I'm asking myself why you aren't in school."

Jordan sighed. "All right." He reached into his pocket.

The policeman took a step back. "Don't do anything silly!"

Realizing that the officer thought he was about to produce a weapon, he said, "Nothing silly about my ID." He held it out, hoping that this particular policeman knew the secret code in the first four digits.

The officer took one look at it and then gazed at Jordan. "Is this some sort of joke?"

"No."

Red-faced, he returned Jordan's ID. "I thought that code was a myth, but apparently not. You really exist."

Jordan smiled. "Yes, I exist. Just."

He walked away with the "Get Out of Jail Free" card in his pocket.

He went through the boatyard and took the track onto the grassy headland. There he stopped and scanned the harbour. Ben Smith had not taken an interest in boats, but they seemed to be dominating Jordan Stryker's life. First, there was the SS *Richard Montgomery*. Then there was Cara Quickfall's tiny motorboat that catalysed the explosion. An oil supertanker and *Ocean Courage* made everything so much worse. And now there was Hoo Marina.

Somewhere near these moorings, Mr. Bool had made his final phone call and then disappeared. What had happened to him? Had he simply sailed away? There was no point asking if one of the marina's boats had gone missing. The estuary explosion had caused a surge of water down the Medway and one of the bombs from the *Richard Montgomery* had landed here. Quite a few boats had been lost.

Beyond some workshops, an impact crater marked the position where the WW2 bomb had hit, seventy years late. On either side of the muddy footpath, small boats were lolling on the ground as if the area was a boats' graveyard. Some were covered in tarpaulins, many were bare and rotting, others were burned out. The ones that had been reduced to wooden frames looked like discarded skeletons.

In the river, on the side that led to the Thames Estuary, three rusting wrecks rested on the bottom.

Experts, like detectives and forensic scientists, would

probably examine the scene and read the signs of what had happened here. A disturbance of the earth might suggest a scuffle had taken place. Stains in a particular pattern could reveal a certain type of attack. But Jordan couldn't do any of that clever stuff. Sitting down on the mud, he hoped he had other strengths to offer. Within minutes, he heard a group of boys in the distance.

Jordan watched as they approached. There were about ten of them and most were older than him. More like young men than boys. Two were talking on mobiles. They were definitely not the friendly bunch he'd expected. He didn't recognize any of them as schoolmates from a year earlier. And he got the impression that they were annoyed to see an outsider on their patch. Times had clearly changed.

"Hiya," said Jordan, as brightly as he could.

"What are you doing here?"

"Nothing. Just hanging out." Jordan's plan to mix with the crowd until he could steer the talk onto stolen mobiles and schoolteachers was falling to pieces before it began.

"Don't go near him," one of them cried. "I've got bruises that prove he's dangerous."

"He's a kid!"

"He can bust doors and stop bullets with his hand."

The others laughed.

"Yeah?" someone else said in a mocking tone. "And my baby brother wrestles tigers."

"I'm not joking!"

Jordan didn't recognize him but he must have been among the dealers at the sports club.

The guy was not going to give in to ridicule. "The boss said she wanted to sort him out. I'm calling her." He put his phone to his ear.

The mood changed instantly. At the mention of the boss, there was no more joshing. The others seemed to realize that calling Melissa Pink meant this business was deadly serious.

Jordan rose to his feet and almost all of them took a step back. The nervy one from the sports centre trained a gun on him. "Make a run for it and I'll put a bullet in your back. You won't stop that with your hand."

The sudden appearance of a gun took the tension to another level. Jordan held his breath.

"Let's take him to the shed."

The dealer with the gun waved it in the direction of a long windowless shack with a corrugated plastic roof. It was an outbuilding for storing and maintaining boats. Four of the young men led the way and the rest – including the guy with the gun – stayed behind Jordan. This time,

Jordan couldn't see a way to escape from Melissa Pink's heavies. He entered the workshop.

Inside, it could have been the set of a horror film. It was lit by a flickering fluorescent tube. There were workbenches along both sides. Tools and parts of boats littered the place. There were chains and ropes everywhere. At the far end there was a pool filled with a dirty liquid. The smell coming from it was evil.

The thugs formed a circle around him.

"Now we wait," the gangster with the gun said. "She won't be long."

Melissa Pink was an unremarkable and compact woman. She was in her late thirties, Jordan guessed, but she was the height of a twelve-year-old. Her freckly face was pale and her long ginger hair was probably natural. She wasn't carrying a weapon but both of her muscular minders were armed under their jackets. One of them was the bald man with the bushy beard who had tried to shoot Jordan in the sports centre.

"What have we here?" Melissa said with a smile. "A freak, I think." Keeping at least one pace away from him, she walked right around him. She reminded Jordan of a vulture checking out a carcass before pouncing and tearing off pieces of flesh. She came to a halt on his right and gazed at the fake hand. "The bionic boy, no less. What's your name?"

"Jordan."

"Jordan what?"

"Stryker."

She continued her circuit until she faced him again. "You roughed up my club. Why?"

"Your bouncers tried to rough me up," Jordan answered. "I was defending myself."

"Have you been to the police about what you saw?"

"No."

Melissa stared at him coldly. "Who are you working for?"

"I'm fourteen. I don't work for anyone."

"No one official maybe." She sniffed noisily. "What does the name Goss mean to you?"

Her question took him by surprise. "Er... Nothing."

She laughed. "Bionic and transparent."

"I mean, I'm not working for him."

"Yes, you are," she replied, scratching her nose.

Jordan's legs were trembling. He fought to keep control. He wondered if he would be better off letting her believe that he worked for her gangland rival. If he persuaded her that she was wrong, she might demand answers he would not dare to reveal. He didn't deny it again.

"If I got close enough," she asked, "could you crush my arm – or my neck?"

He nodded. "Easily."

"Hmm." Sneering, she said, "I wonder what you're worth in scrap metal."

Her henchmen sniggered. They probably knew what was on her mind. Perhaps it was also compulsory to acknowledge her clever remarks.

Saying as little as possible wasn't helping Jordan to cope with his situation – or with his nerves. He changed tactics. "Can I ask you something?"

She shrugged. "It makes no difference."

Jordan didn't like the sound of that. He shuddered but carried on anyway. "Did you set off the estuary explosion?"

She laughed cruelly. "Neat operation."

"But was it you?"

"Doesn't Goss know? I'd like to claim it but, no, it wasn't one of mine." She was a restless and fidgety woman. She removed some wax from her ear with her little finger, flicked it off, and then continued. "Canvey Arms Factory copped it. Ask yourself why. There's some stupid people around here who don't like war, guns and bombs. Anti-war protesters." She shook her head as if she felt sorry for them. "They think we should all hold hands and be nice to each other instead of making weapons. Believe me, you don't have to look much further to find out who did it. They wanted to whip up a backlash against the arms trade." Putting on a high-pitched voice, she said, "Now you've seen the harm that bombs do, let's make sure this country never builds any more. Peace and love."

"You sound sure."

"It's what I've heard. But if Goss – and everyone else – thinks I did it... Good. It serves a purpose. It reminds them not to mess with Melissa Pink. Fear works."

Jordan didn't know this woman, but he thought she might be telling the truth.

She gave another of her ugly smiles. "You know, if we were in a film, this is the scene where I say, 'I could use a lad like you.' I'd offer you power and money to leave Goss and work for me. But it's not a film. I just want you out of my way and off my territory." She glanced at the pool of foul liquid at the end of the shed.

Jordan followed her gaze fearfully.

"It's caustic. It strips paint off metal – and flesh off bones." She sniffed loudly again. "Put yourself in my place. I've got my reputation to think of. I can't have a boy questioning – even undermining – my authority around here, so I have to deal with dissent. And it has to be known I deal harshly with dissent. Very harshly. I'm bound to make an example of someone who tries to rough up my club or my people. On top of that, you know too much about me and my business interests. You've seen too much." She looked around her gang of young men and then pointed to the caustic pool. "Get on with it." She began to leave but hesitated. "After you're done," she added, "drain the tank and send the arm back to Goss."

10 PRISON

In horror, Jordan watched Melissa Pink walk out with her silent bodyguards. Presumably she wanted to be able to claim that she wasn't around when the murder took place.

A leering member of the gang came up to Jordan. "Let's have some fun."

Jordan could sense temperature with his infrared vision, he could crush almost anything with his powerful right arm, he could pick up sounds and smells well beyond normal human senses, but he didn't stand a chance against a bullet fired from behind into his back.

"Move. Over there." The gunman waved the weapon towards the stinking pool.

Jordan could have sent a message to Unit Red's computer system with his BCI, but Angel and Winter were in London. They wouldn't be able to send help quickly enough to save him.

Even with an enhanced body, Jordan felt feeble. He stumbled forward until he stood at the edge of the tank and looked down at the corrosive fluid. It was almost black and appeared to be as thick as oil. The lump in his throat made it hard to swallow.

Someone said, "A jump or a push? The choice is yours."

Their brutality made Jordan angry. And anger gave him strength. He refused to believe he'd come through a year of torture to die in this miserable place in such an awful way. "Neither."

"A bullet, then?"

"I'll do it my own way." Holding his breath, he squatted down by the paint stripper as if he was preparing himself to slide into the disgusting pool. But he didn't. He had one chance. He dipped his cupped right hand into the liquid. In one swift movement, he spun round and flung the stuff towards the gangster with the gun. A shower of drops hurtled towards his head. The young man squealed, dropped the gun and covered his face with his arms.

Jordan didn't wait. He plunged his hand into the bath again, scooped out more fluid and flung it at the thugs who were standing between him and the door. Two of them screamed as the spray stung their eyes and bare skin. The others tried to protect themselves by turning their backs or shielding their faces. One yanked off his shirt because the splattered drops had begun to burn through the material. All of them shut their eyes.

Jordan took off. He ran to the door and burst through before any of the gangsters recovered enough to chase him. He dashed past the boats, the café and the entrance. He didn't stop. He sprinted breathlessly into the housing estate. He didn't know the area very well, but he zigzagged through it to put off anyone who might try to follow him. At the edge of the estate that was furthest from the marina, he found himself in The Copse. But it was a dead end. To conceal himself from Pink's heavies, he sidled through the bushes and collapsed among the trees.

There, he went online and left a message. *Emergency. Collect me from The Copse, Hoo. Armed thugs not far away, looking for me.*

He rested against a tree trunk and examined his right-hand side. His shirtsleeve was dissolving and small holes had appeared in his trousers. Underneath, his leg tingled. The artificial skin stretched over his arm had turned orangey-brown and, as he watched, it was still darkening. He hoped the paint stripper wouldn't go right through.

"More damage to government property," he muttered to himself.

As his heart slowed and breathing became easier, he wished for Winter to come early.

In the underground medical room of the Highgate Village house, Jordan sat in the chair that looked like a dentist's. With trays of tools at hand, a technician was peeling back the blackened skin from his arm. "It's called degloving," she told him.

He knew why. It was like removing a very tight and stretchy glove. "Is the metal underneath okay?"

"It's fine. It'll cope with a lot worse than caustic solutions."

Interrupting, Angel said, "But don't try it. A bullet and paint stripper's quite enough." He sat down opposite his youngest agent. "So, you think Melissa Pink could be out of the picture. And she thinks it was peace protesters, but she didn't have any evidence."

"Yes."

Even when Angel was sitting down, his stature was striking. Jordan would've liked to see him next to Melissa Pink. They would have made a comical mismatch. Opposites in height, opposites in law.

Winter chipped in, "And you didn't get anything more on Salam Bool?"

"No."

"You won't give up, though," said Angel.

Jordan never did. For one thing, he was alive. Even when ten thugs had been on the verge of pushing him into a pool of corrosive fluid at gunpoint, Jordan hadn't surrendered.

The technician looked like a nurse as she attended to Jordan's arm, but really she was an engineer. She could have been repairing a dented car left at her service centre. Finishing the de-gloving, she cast the damaged silicone sleeve aside.

Looking at it, Jordan imagined his fake arm was a snake that had just shed its skin.

"Okay," she said. "A wash of the casing, then I'm going to put the spare on."

Angel gave her a slight nod before announcing to

Jordan, "And I'm going to send you to prison tomorrow."

Jordan stared at him. "What?"

"Well, a Young Offender Institution attached to Chelmsford Prison."

"Why?"

"Because there's a prisoner I want you to meet. An arms trade protester who's inside for trying to set fire to a missile base. Name of Gideon Riley. Apparently, everyone calls him Giddy. He's high profile in the anti-war movement. He'll know if that's what the estuary explosion was all about. To pass the time, he's formed a group – he plays guitar – but he's about to lose his drummer."

"How do you know?"

"Because I'm getting him moved to a different prison. You can help Riley with the gap in his band."

"You know about me and drums?"

"If I didn't, I wouldn't be doing my job properly."

Jordan wasn't surprised, but he was dismayed. He knew very little about Angel, but Angel knew everything about him. To Jordan, that felt wrong. And creepy. He wanted to have secrets. Without them, he wasn't his own person. He might as well belong to Unit Red. He promised himself he'd keep some secrets from Angel and Winter. Including Amy Goss.

"You've gone quiet," said Angel. "What are you thinking about?"

"Nothing," Jordan replied. "I was just wondering what I'm supposed to do with Gideon Riley – apart from join his band."

Angel shrugged. "Make friends. Gain his trust. Let him talk. You just have to listen."

"And hope he mentions blowing up the *Richard Montgomery*?"

"Or convinces you he didn't. As soon as you find out, you'll get early release."

Jordan nodded. "That reminds me. What am I supposed to have done to get banged up in the first place?"

Angel laughed. "I'll think of something."

The technician rolled the artificial skin right up to Jordan's reconstructed shoulder and said, "There you are. As good as new." She smiled oddly at Angel and added, "Everything's in place."

It was Friday 20th April and Jordan was letting rip in the recreation room when Prisoner 1345 took an interest in his drumming. Under the watchful eyes of the guards, the man leaned on the pool table for a while before coming forward. "You're pretty good," he said.

"I used to be." Jordan held out his artificial arm. "This doesn't help."

"Still sounds cool to me."

"Thanks."

"They call me Giddy," he said. "What are you in for?"

"I've got a habit of setting fire to things. They said I'm doing it to get my own back for my accident."

"Are you?"

Jordan shrugged. "I just like flames."

He couldn't ever remember being so untruthful when he was plain Ben Smith. Then again, he was trying not to dredge up his past. He guessed that being a secret agent was always going to involve deception.

Giddy didn't seem to sense any threat in the young offender. "What's your name?" he asked.

"Jordan."

"And what are you going to do when you get out?"

"How do you mean?"

"More arson?"

Jordan shrugged again.

"You're young. You don't want to come back here. It's not a nice place to be."

Jordan had learned that already. It was depressing. Everywhere he looked there were tall wire fences, locked doors, and prison guards. The place was a relentless grey. The loudest sounds were barked commands and slamming gates. Everything happened slowly. Everyone walked at a snail's pace. Nothing was worth running for. He spent a large part of every day in queues. Queues for food, queues to go through doors, queues to be frisked, queues for the showers. Queues for everything. Prison erased choice and personality. Most of all, it was miserable because the prisoners couldn't just pack up and leave whenever they needed a break from life inside.

"After you've done your time, keep to drumsticks," Giddy said. "Stay clear of matchsticks."

"I'll try."

"Perhaps I can help."

"Oh?"

"How do you fancy playing in a band?"

It felt good to be thumping out a rhythm again, but it wasn't with the same joy. He was drumming as part of a mission, he felt as if his strong right arm was about to thrust the stick straight through the skin and, like most nervous drummers, he speeded up the beat too much.

Taking a break from rehearsals, drinking a weird

liquid that was supposed to be tea, Jordan asked Giddy, "What are you in for?"

"Playing guitar very badly."

"Seriously."

Giddy smiled. "Not so different from what you did. They got me for setting fire to a military camp. Not for the first time."

"Why?"

"I don't like the arms industry."

Jordan played dumb. Puzzled, he looked down at his artificial arm.

Giddy's expression was part amusement, part annoyance. "No. Not that sort of arms industry. *Arms*. Missiles, bombs, guns and stuff."

"Oh. Right." Jordan paused before adding, "What's the problem with them?"

"What's the problem?" he exclaimed. "They kill people. That's what." He started waving his hands around and nearly knocked over his tea. "Bombs are what go off in the Middle East or wherever. Not England. Not usually anyway. We're divorced from it. We don't understand what it's like. We don't have to hide in basements and hope. We don't have to bury victims. We've forgotten the reality of war. We make weapons and sell them all over the place, but don't see the result."

Jordan nodded. "I used to live near Canvey Arms Factory. It's not there any more. It went up in the estuary explosion."

"Good," Giddy said.

Jordan looked into his face. "You didn't... Did you?"

"Set it off?" Giddy shook his head. "No. But I'm glad someone did, because it taught us all a lesson. It brought home the havoc and destruction our bombs cause."

"People died."

Giddy gazed at Jordan. "Yeah. I'm sorry about that."

"You can't be the only anti-bomb protester. Did one of your mates do it?"

"Bombs set off by people campaigning against bombs. Does that sound very likely to you?"

Jordan shrugged.

"A few of them claimed it, but I'd know if any of them did it." Giddy shook his head and got to his feet. "No chance. Come on. I've written a song about it. 'Arms Trade'. You'll like it. It's fast and furious. Suits your style. Let's give it a go."

Jordan knew that Gideon Riley would be kept in prison for a lot longer if he was convicted of the estuary explosion. So it was in his interests to deny that he was responsible. Jordan also suspected that he might keep quiet to protect one of his campaigning friends.

But Giddy had no reason to believe that Jordan – apparently a young offender – would tell the authorities about their conversation. Jordan thought he was probably telling the truth.

As far as Jordan was concerned, he'd done the job. He could do no more. Being locked up for five days was quite enough. He played one gig with Giddy's band for the inmates before he exchanged a cell in jail for a small bedroom above the dead of Highgate Cemetery. Getting out of prison was like being able to breathe freely again. He was no longer confined, even if he was still trapped within Unit Red.

11 HERO

Jordan was still puzzled by Mr. Bool's suspicious behaviour. He wanted to get to the bottom of it. There was an obvious way to try for more information, but it made him feel edgy. He'd decided to speak to Amy again. He wanted to find out if she'd heard anything about the teacher and his stolen phone since the explosion.

Jordan didn't tell Winter that he was planning to speak to Amy Goss. He admitted only that he was going to Salam Bool's school. Before he set out, Winter said,

"You've got to be careful around Medway now. Very careful. Melissa Pink and her people will be gunning for you in a big way." She was bound to be right and her warning increased his tension.

Aiming to reach the school for the end of the last lesson, Jordan kept glancing round as he walked along the main road through Hoo.

Ahead of him, something was happening. It looked as if a car had spun off the road and slammed into a tree. Small flames were dancing around under the car, threatening an explosion at any moment. He ran towards the scene of the accident. The driver's door was open and a woman was kneeling beside it, struggling to yank the unconscious driver out.

Jordan went towards her.

"Get back!" she cried. "It's going to blow."

"How do you know?"

"I'm a fire officer. Off duty. Now, get back!"

"But he's wedged in."

"Yes. By the steering wheel."

"I'll move it." Jordan went round to the passenger's door, opened it and lay across the front seats. They felt unnaturally warm. He put his right arm next to the driver's legs and prepared himself to strike upwards at the steering column.

"Don't," the firefighter said. "It's metal. Too strong. You'll hurt yourself."

Jordan ignored her. He rammed his arm into the steering column as hard as he could. But the blow didn't shift it. He hit it again in the same place and this time it budged a fraction of a centimetre. Nowhere near enough to make a difference.

Jordan's third strike bent the steering column but it was still jammed against the driver's chest.

Jordan could feel heat on his feet and ankles as they dangled outside. The flames were rising. The whole car was baking. He broke into a sweat. He probably had time for one more attempt.

He took a deep breath, steeled himself and then walloped the column again. This time, it gave way and the steering wheel jerked a few centimetres away from the driver. Adjusting his position, Jordan gripped the wheel in his metal fist and pushed it towards the shattered windscreen to give more clearance.

"That's it!" the fire officer shouted. Ignoring the man's injuries – she didn't have time to protect any broken bones – she grabbed him under his arms and dragged him out.

Jordan got up and dashed round to the other side. He took the wounded man's legs and helped to lift him away to safety. Together, they staggered a distance from the crashed car.

The woman stopped and lowered the driver's shoulders carefully to the pavement.

Jordan did the same with his legs.

"I don't know how you did that," the firefighter said breathlessly, "but thanks." Then she looked closely into Jordan's eyes and gasped. "I know you, don't I?"

Jordan froze for a moment. He'd never seen her before. "No, I don't think so."

"Who are you?" she asked.

"No one."

Then she gazed at his artificial arm and it all clicked into place. "I remember," she said. "It was a priority address in Shepherds Way. Something to do with the police..."

Behind Jordan, the car exploded. The fire officer put her arm in front of her face to protect her eyes and Jordan used the opportunity. He darted away as fast as he could.

He was just out of sight of the burning wreck when he ran into several packs of school kids. Some were rushing towards him, keen to find out what had caused the blast.

"Hey! Watch where you're going!" somebody shouted at him.

"Sorry," he muttered.

Somewhere in the distance, several sirens screeched. Police car, fire engine and ambulance, Jordan guessed. The confused wailing was getting louder.

Slowing to a walk, he merged with the crowds of students and got his breath back. Trying to ignore what had just happened, he went in the direction of Lower Stoke. He knew that was the way Amy would go.

He saw her first from the back. He wasn't sure how he knew it was Amy Goss, but he was certain. Her hair was different. Shorter. She was taller. Maybe slightly taller than he was. Jordan recalled that she could put food away with great gusto. In an effort to stay trim, she always ordered a Diet Coke with her double cheeseburger and large fries.

Most of the students were strolling away from school in small noisy groups, but Amy walked alone. Jordan felt an overwhelming urge to befriend her, just as he'd done years earlier.

He speeded up until he drew level with her. "Hi," he said. "You're the girl I met the other night by the silo."

Amy looked him up and down. "Jordan."

"That's right. You didn't say your name."

"How did you know it was me?"

"My mum made me eat lots of carrots when I was little."

She smiled briefly. "So you can see in the dark."

"Actually, I heard you talking to someone back there. I recognized your voice."

Amy's face creased. "Are you stalking me or something? Because, if you are, I should tell you I've got a pretty heavy family. You wouldn't stand a chance."

Jordan read something different in her moody eyes. No matter what she said, she knew that her family wasn't so heavy any more.

A bunch of girls brushed past and one called out, "Caught yourself a live one this time?"

Amy scowled at the group and then ignored them.

Jordan ran his left hand through his thick black hair. He'd let it grow long to hide the bumps on his head and because Ben Smith had always kept it short. "I cut my last lesson so I could come and find you."

"Why?" She hesitated before adding, "If you say you like the sound of my voice, I'm going to scream till you get arrested."

"You're funny."

"You're avoiding the question."

Jordan remembered a thirteen-year-old bundle of fun, a girl who distrusted any form of authority, a girl who spoke her mind. Now, he sensed that she was even more blunt. She also seemed less mischievous. There was an air of sadness about her. The river blast had probably taken its toll.

Despite his nerves, Jordan grinned. "Did you know a teacher called Salam Bool?"

Amy stopped in her tracks.

"I take that as a yes," said Jordan. "I know he taught at your school. You see, he lives next door to me. Or at least he did."

"Everyone says he died in the explosion."

"Round my way, they just say he's missing. His house is still empty, waiting for him to come back. If he ever does."

"What's this got to do with me?" Amy asked.

"By those silos, you said something about school and it reminded me of him. I just wondered if you knew anything."

"Why are the bottoms of your trousers all burned?"

"Are they?" Jordan looked down. She was right. They'd been scorched. "Did you hear the sirens a few minutes ago?" he said. "There was an accident just down the road. I helped to pull a man from a burning car."

"Are you telling me I'm talking to a hero?"

He shook his head. "I just lent a hand."

Amy stopped again and turned to face him. "What's up with your hand anyway? And your whole arm."

"That was another car crash. You don't want to know the details. I got fitted with a false one."

Amy nodded. "Is that why you dash off to help someone in a pile-up?"

"I guess so."

"I do know something about Mr. Bool," she said, "but why should I trust you?"

He shrugged. "No idea."

"At least that's honest."

Jordan waited. He hoped that she could still detect in him whatever she'd liked in Ben Smith.

Amy took a deep breath. "I don't know why, but there's something about you. I suppose I trust you enough."

Inside, Jordan was screaming, *I'm a complete fraud*. Ben Smith wouldn't have lied to her. But Jordan Stryker was finding it easier and easier to be underhand as his mission progressed. What had he become? He knew, of course. He'd become a Unit Red agent. He wanted to be Amy's friend, but he was using her instead.

"Just before Bool disappeared – just before the big blast – someone nicked his mobile. I didn't know who'd done it at the time. A lot of people thought it was me, but it wasn't. It was a boy called Ed Hathaway. His mates gave the game away afterwards." Amy shook her head at the hopelessness of boys. "Mind you, when I saw him, he wasn't showing off about what he'd done. He said he was going to make some silly calls with it, but he spotted these weird messages."

"What weird messages?"

She shrugged. "I don't know really. Ed said they looked like wanted posters. A photo of someone and an amount of money. Anyway, he was messing around with it when it rang. Mr. Bool was just round the corner on another mobile. This was at the marina. Ed was with his crazy mates and brothers. Obviously, Mr. Bool knew some of the lads hung out there and he was checking if they'd got his phone. Right in one." She began to walk along the road again.

Jordan caught up with her and asked, "What happened?"

"You can guess. You're a boy. How do boys and men solve anything? There was a lot of shouting, pushing, pulling and hitting."

"And?"

Amy shrugged again. "That's it. Ed and his mates ran off. I don't know what happened to Mr. Bool. Or to his phone."

"If I want to know any more, I'd better see Ed Hathaway."

"Not easy," Amy replied.

"Why?"

"He left."

"Where did he go?"

"Newcastle."

"Newcastle?"

"It's a city up north," Amy said dryly. "Even further north than Luton."

Trying to behave like a normal boy again, he replied, "I didn't know there was anything north of Luton, apart from the North Pole."

"I'm going now," Amy announced, pointing to a lane on the right. "On my own."

Jordan came to a halt on the pavement. "Okay."

Just before she dashed across the road, she smiled at him and said, "I'm Amy, by the way."

He shouted after her, "See you around, Amy."

When Jordan reported back to Unit Red, he told Angel and Winter that he'd gathered his information about Salam Bool by talking to a group of school kids. He didn't mention Amy. When he also told them about the car crash and the firefighter, he noticed that they exchanged a glance.

At once, Angel began to tap his computer keypad.

Winter said, "So, my guess is you want an outing to Newcastle to see this Ed Hathaway."

Jordan nodded. "Yes."

"I'll find out where he lives or which school he goes to."

"Thanks."

Angel looked up from his screen. "I've got a recording I want you to listen to."

"What is it?"

"When Ben Smith's house collapsed, it was a female firefighter who found him," Angel answered. "There aren't many women in the local fire brigade so I'm putting two and two together... But, I could be wrong. This is the recording of the rescue. Listen and tell me if you recognize her voice." He hit the *return* key.

Firefighter: Fourteen Shepherds Way – with parts of sixteen, I think – Lower Stoke. Just awful. Too close to the blast.
Control: Fourteen Shepherds Way is a priority address. A police officer's house. DS Smith. According to records, she wasn't on duty. She was probably in bed.

F.F.: I'm sorry. It's a war zone down here. No one's alive.

There was a pause in the exchange. Jordan nodded and said, "Yes. That's her."

"Thought so."

Angel was about to turn off the sound file when Jordan put out his hand and said, "No. Let me hear what happened. Please."

"All right."

F.F.: Just a second.
C.: What is it? Do you want medical assistance?
F.F.: I don't think so. False alarm. It's a boy. He's dead. I just hope he went quickly.
C.: Move on.
F.F.: No. I want medical backup.
C.: What? Do you have signs of life?
F.F.: I thought he just moved.
C.: Are you sure?
F.F.: Yes. Quick. Get a resuscitation team in here.

The recording ended but Jordan couldn't speak. He felt completely churned up inside.

"You couldn't possibly have moved," Angel said. "She lied for some reason."

"She's another one who doesn't give up," Winter remarked.

Jordan found his voice again. "She saved my life! What's her name?"

"You don't need to know," Angel replied.

"I should thank her."

Angel shook his head. "No, you can't. Ben died, remember. It's very...awkward that she recognized you."

"But she's a hero."

"Yes," Angel agreed. "Hero *and* security risk."

12 DEBTS

"Are you Ed Hathaway?" Really, Jordan didn't need to ask. Ed still looked like the boy who had been in Ben Smith's class a year earlier. He had the same short silvery hair, pinched face and roguish appearance. But there was no sign of his once frothy nature.

"Maybe."

"It's all right," Jordan replied, "I won't tell anyone what you did in Hoo Marina."

Wide-eyed, Ed exclaimed, "What? Who are you?"

"Jordan. I'm trying to find out what happened to Salam Bool. You'll remember Mr. Bool."

Ed's cheeks glowed red. His mouth opened, but he didn't say anything.

Behind Ed were the tall white railings that ran right around his new school. Jordan wasn't sure if the spiked fence was there to keep students in or to keep everyone else out. The area had seen better days. It was the sort of estate where a home-delivered pizza would arrive faster than an ambulance.

"Tell me, and that'll be the end of it," said Jordan.

"You're not a mate of his, are you? Or in his family?"

Jordan shook his head and smiled. "Nothing like. My mum fell out with him over money. Something about gambling. She's been trying to find him and get her own back for a year now."

"She'll be lucky," Ed muttered.

Jordan shrugged. "She's threatening to go to the police with what we already know. And it won't sound good. You took his phone, had a fight with him, and no one's seen him since. The cops'll be round your place, kicking the door in. Not like us. We just want your side of the story."

"Why isn't she here?" he said, looking around.

"Working. She thought it'd be easier for me to talk to

you because we're the same sort of age."

There was some truth in Jordan's answer. He was exploiting his natural advantage over the police. Already, he'd got further than the official investigation into Mr. Bool because he was the right age to chat to young people like Amy. He hoped it was going to work on Ed Hathaway as well. Of course, he also had the advantage of knowing about the teacher's missing mobile phone in the first place.

"But..."

"Did you come up here to Newcastle to get away from what you did?"

"I told Mum. She thought it'd be best..." He stopped and stared at Jordan. "Look. I don't know why I'm telling you this. I didn't do anything. Not really."

"You nicked his mobile."

"That was just a prank," Ed replied.

"But it went wrong."

"Me and my brothers were going to have fun with it. We were going to phone his home number."

"Dangerous. He was a big bloke, not the fun type really."

"Yeah, well. He put me in detention and it wasn't my fault. That's why I was getting my own back. But the phone started ringing. Lots of times. Next thing, he was right on top of us. We didn't attack him. He attacked us. He was mad. Wanted his phone back."

"What happened?"

Ed sighed. "We never meant... We were just defending ourselves. I pushed him away and he tripped over a rope. That's all. No knives or anything."

"And?"

"He bashed his head on one of those things you tie boats to."

Jordan winced. "I bet that hurt."

"More than that."

"What? You mean, it killed him?"

"I think so."

"How do you know?"

Ed grimaced. "He didn't look good."

"What did you do?"

He hesitated. "Will your mum really go to the police if I don't tell you?"

Jordan nodded. "She's like that."

"All right," Ed replied. He took a deep breath. "We were scared in case we got blamed for killing him. We were bound to. Boys always get the blame. So we covered it up. We shoved him in an old leaky boat and pushed it out into the river. We thought it'd sink. I didn't hear anything afterwards about him being found so I guess it worked. He must have gone down with it. Maybe waves from the explosion swamped the boat if it didn't sink on its own."

Jordan had survived a similar wound to the head – and worse – but he'd been given expert medical attention. He hadn't been pushed out in a boat and left for dead. "What did you do with his phone?" Jordan asked.

"I threw it in the boat. It went with him."

"Shame."

"Why?"

"Because you found something on it, didn't you? Pictures and stuff."

"Yes," Ed answered.

"What was that all about?"

"Not a clue."

"Come on," Jordan said. "You don't forget when you've just killed someone and dumped his body."

"I didn't kill him. I didn't mean to."

"Okay. But tell me what you saw on his mobile."

Ed took a moment to think. "There was a picture of this bloke, something about five thousand pounds and where he lived."

"What was his name?"

"It was a long time ago."

Jordan simply stared at Ed and waited.

"Can't remember his first name. His last name was Dodd or Dowd or something, I think."

"Where did he live?"

"I remember that because I've got an uncle there. It was somewhere in Peterborough."

"What was his address?"

Ed exclaimed, "You've got to be kidding!"

"All right."

Jordan thought the key words of *Dodd*, *Dowd*, *Peterborough* and *money* into the Unit Red computer, but the search did not bring up anything significant.

Clearly surprised by Jordan's sudden silence, Ed prompted, "Well? I don't know any more."

"Sorry. I was thinking."

"What happens now?" Ed asked him.

"Nothing. If you've given me all you've got."

Ed raised both arms, palms upward, indicating that he had no more.

"Okay," said Jordan. "Thanks."

"You won't dump me in it?"

"No," Jordan promised. "I'm only interested in Salam Bool." He turned his back on Ed and headed for the railway station.

On his way to Newcastle Central, Jordan called Unit Red to report on his exchange with Ed Hathaway. Angel didn't know what to make of the contents of Mr. Bool's phone either, but he promised to search through databases for information on a man called Dodd or Dowd in Peterborough. He also promised to persuade a police team to look for Bool's body.

The train trundled across one of the impressive bridges over the River Tyne. Drumming his fingers on the table, Jordan viewed the series of huge iron and concrete structures, but he was thinking about the missing Mr. Bool. Jordan had never really imagined any teacher having a life outside of school so it had been a shock to find out that Mr. Bool was an obsessive gambler, mixed up with a shady loan company. He remembered that the teacher had not been in school on the morning of the missing phone and the Thames explosion. Perhaps he was placing bets or working on some money-making scheme.

The rumbling sound in the carriage changed as the train returned to solid ground and accelerated. Less interested in the industrial scenes out of the window, Jordan opened a file in his mind on the casualties of the estuary blast. He scanned down the lists for all deaths that had occurred in boats. He wanted to know if every victim had been identified beyond doubt or whether one might have been Salam Bool.

It was a depressing task. The register began with the crew of *Ocean Courage*. Not one of the thirty had survived. Twenty-eight of the badly burned bodies had been found in the wreckage of the ship. Two more had been recovered from the estuary. The captain's death was particularly sad, Jordan thought, because the voyage was his first in charge of the huge ship.

Six people in small boats had made it back to the shore. Two had not. Both of the drowned bodies had been identified by next of kin. A married couple in one of Southend's marinas had become trapped when their yacht submerged. The river police officers who had chased Cara Quickfall's motor-launch had died when their patrol boat went down. Four shift workers unloading oil at Canvey Island had died on the supertanker when it went up in flames.

Jordan saw nothing to suggest that one of these victims might have been Mr. Bool, wrongly identified as someone else. It seemed likely that what remained of his body was still in the river somewhere – or maybe it had been swept out to sea and lost for ever.

As the train powered south, not far from York, Angel called. "I want you to get off at Peterborough," he said.

"Why?"

"Because I've found a man called Vinnie Dowd. He still lives there. Winter will meet you at the station and take you to him."

"Why me? Winter could do it on her own, couldn't she?"

"Yes, but I'm not sure she'd be as successful. Vinnie Dowd might sympathize more with someone else who's been disfigured."

Keeping his voice down, Jordan said, "He's been disfigured?"

"That's how I found him. His hospital record says someone threw acid over him, same day as the *Richard Montgomery* went up."

"That's horrible. Why?"

"Over to you and Winter. But it's worth pointing out that Bool taught chemistry, didn't he?"

"Yes."

"So he knows all about acid and no doubt he had access to it at school."

"But..." Jordan stopped. He didn't understand why Mr. Bool would do something like that. He didn't know why Angel was suggesting that he might have done it.

"I've got a theory," Angel said. "Winter'll bring a photo of Salam Bool. Show it to Dowd and see if he recognizes him. Then we'll know."

* * *

Jordan and Winter found Vinnie Dowd pottering about in the tidy back garden of his small terraced house in a rundown suburb of Peterborough. He was blind in his left eye and much of that side of his face had been burned. Surgery had repaired it as much as possible, but it certainly wasn't a pretty sight. For Vinnie's sake – and for his own – Jordan hoped that people looked beyond surface blemishes.

Glancing round the garden, Jordan introduced himself and then asked, "Hey. Do you keep chickens down there, where it's wired off?"

Vinnie looked him up and down, lingering on his face and artificial arm. "Yes. But, even round here, the foxes get them."

"We had some once," he replied. "A long time ago. And it was the same thing. But I guess foxes are just doing what they do."

"What do you want?"

"I looked you up. Found out what happened to you. I've come to see if you can help me."

"Me? Help you? What is this?"

"I'm trying to find out who attacked you. Did you see him?"

Vinnie took a deep breath before he answered. "Yes, I saw him. Just a flash, but I won't forget."

"Can you look at a photo and tell me if it's him?"

"Yes. But..."

"What?"

"I know who did it."

Puzzled, Jordan asked, "Who?"

"Well, I owe money..."

"Who to?"

"He calls himself *EasyCash*. He sent one of his men. When I couldn't pay..." He touched the ragged parts of his face. "It's a reminder to keep up the payments."

Jordan grimaced. "Did you report it to the police?"

"What's the point? And I don't want them looking into where my money comes from – or how I spend it." He glanced at Winter and asked, "You're not police, are you?"

Winter laughed and shook her head.

Looking back at Jordan, Vinnie said, "Did he do your arm in as well? Is that why you're after him?"

"I'd like to know who did this to me. More than that. I need to know." He turned towards Winter and she held out the photo of Salam Bool.

Immediately, Vinnie nodded.

"Sure?"

"Certain."

It didn't make sense to Jordan. Vinnie and Mr. Bool should have been on the same side. They both owed money to *EasyCash OnLine*. "Thanks," he said. "That's all I need."

"What's his name?"

"Salam Bool. He's a teacher. Or was. We're pretty sure he died in the Thames explosion a year back, straight after he saw you."

"Good."

"At least he can't do it to anyone else. But..."

"What?"

"One thing's puzzling me. He owed *EasyCash* a lot of money as well."

Vinnie looked faintly surprised, but then smiled and nodded. "When you're in debt and the devil's after you, you'll agree to anything."

"What? You mean..."

"There's more than one way to pay it back. He couldn't cough up enough so I bet he agreed to extract money from other people in the same boat – like me."

Jordan was horrified that Vinnie almost seemed to accept that this was the way the world worked. Jordan also wondered how many other clients had ended up in hospital because of Salam Bool.

If Mr. Bool had become a vicious debt collector, it explained why he'd destroyed the messages on his computer and hunted down his missing mobile. They could have given him away. And the final recording on his home phone made sense. *"I hear you've done the job. I'll be in touch."* It was probably *EasyCash* acknowledging the success of Mr. Bool's latest – and last – contract. Perhaps Ed Hathaway had unknowingly done a favour to everyone who got into trouble with the loan company.

Back in the car, Winter said, "Good work. Salam Bool isn't one of our suspects any more. Ed Hathaway gave him an alibi at Hoo Marina. You can't blow anything up when you're unconscious or dead. And all the suspicious stuff – like the landline message and his missing mobile – was about debts, not bombs."

Angel's urgent voice sounded above the hum of the engine, making Jordan jump. "Winter. There's a situation brewing. I want you to turn round and head for Hunstanton."

Winter did not question her chief's order for a moment. She tugged on the steering wheel and executed a perfect U-turn at speed. Jordan was thrown sideways in his seat, the tyres screeched, a horn sounded somewhere, and Winter accelerated in the opposite direction. The engine's hum became a roar as the Audi hurtled north-east.

"On the way," she said calmly into the hands-free phone. "You'd better brief us."

13 CLIFF

"There's a group of political extremists who've smashed up a few banks here in London, brought down some government websites, scrawled slogans across the city, and even kidnapped a businessman for a while," Angel explained. "I've got an undercover agent in there trying to find out if they were responsible for the estuary bomb as well. For the purposes of the mission, he's called Tom Flynn. I know *where* he is. Hunstanton. His GPS chip tells me he's stationary at a supermarket on the edge of the town, but he missed his last two contact times. That means something's wrong. I hope for his sake they haven't worked out who he really is."

"Before he went quiet," Winter said, "what did he find out?"

"Nothing about the estuary bomb, but he said the group's planning a big splash. They're bent on attacking a symbol of capitalism and getting their cause on the news. I don't need to tell you that could mean a hit on a supermarket. Find out what's going on, Winter."

Eyes fixed on the road as she overtook a long line of cars, she replied, "Okay."

Winter spun the wheel, taking the sharp bend past the petrol station and up into the car park. It was large and mostly empty. Bringing the car to a halt at the front of the supermarket, Winter reported, "We've arrived. Is Tom still somewhere here?"

"Yes," Angel's voice replied from the speaker. "He hasn't moved."

"Worrying."

"Take care."

Winter undid her safety belt. "I'm going into the shop to look around," she said to Jordan. "You stay here in

contact with Angel. Watch out for anything unusual."
Without giving him time to reply, she got out, slammed
the door, and strode to the entrance.

As soon as she disappeared inside, everything became
still and quiet. The sky was dull and thick with cloud.
Over the road, there was another parking area, caravans
and houses. Through the drizzle, Jordan could also see
a large carousel and the tops of funfair rides. They
weren't moving, though. They seemed to be closed.
Beyond them was the grey sea. An elderly couple in
heavy coats emerged from the supermarket and shuffled
towards some steps that led up into a housing estate.
Two cars drove past the shop and out of town.

A minute passed. Nothing happened. This part of the
coastal town appeared to be dead.

Then Angel's voice came out of the phone speaker.
"He's moving! Not fast. Just a few metres away from the
building."

Suddenly alert, Jordan looked all around. There was
no sign of movement.

"He's edging towards the road."

Jordan was puzzled. "But nothing's..." He stopped
when he spotted the cab of a truck pulling out of the
delivery area at the back of the supermarket. "Hang on.
It's a lorry!" he said. There was no sign of Winter so he

made a decision. "I'm going after it!"

As he shut the car door, Angel was saying something through the secure phone but Jordan didn't listen. He sprinted along the pavement beside the shop.

Ahead of him, the lorry eased out of the goods entrance and turned right. It was heading away from him, towards the centre of Hunstanton. Jordan was too late to see the driver or to clamber up the passenger's side. The truck gathered speed. Without Winter's help, he had only two options. He could watch it go or he could try and do something about it.

He would risk anything if it helped him solve his first case. Putting on a burst of speed, he ran up to its rear end and jumped onto the back door. Clinging onto a damp handle, he stood on its footplate. The lorry went along the straight road for a short distance, slowed and then forked left. Jordan gripped tighter as it swayed round the corner.

The truck juddered as it went over bumps and drain covers in the road. It seemed to be trying to shake him off. Jordan had no idea how long he would have to hang onto the lorry's tailgate. It could be hours. He decided he had to get inside. Grasping the locked handle tightly with his left hand, he smashed his right fist through the thin metal door. Peeling back the aluminium sheet with his artificial arm, he made a hole big enough to edge through.

Running parallel to the beach, the lorry swerved round a parked car and Jordan's feet slipped off their wet and risky perch. He let out an instinctive scream. He was about to fall heavily into the road when his right hand closed around the torn metal. Hanging from the back of the truck, he heaved himself awkwardly upwards. The strong wind coming off the sea buffeted him. Manoeuvring his top half in through the hole, he pitched forward. The rough edge of the metal was as sharp as an opened tin can. It cut painfully into his skin as his waist and legs followed the rest of him through the gap.

He landed head first on the floor of the trailer and rolled over. His legs slammed against a stack of cardboard boxes. Taking a deep breath, he got to his feet, lurching with the lorry's uneven movement. The trailer wasn't full. It must have delivered most of its load. Some boxes were still strapped to the struts around its sides and there were a few scattered items but there was a lot of space. Inside, the air smelled of everything. He detected fish, tobacco, soaps, vegetables, lots more supermarket goods, and the seaside smell of seaweed. He heard the wind pummelling the side of the truck, the engine growling and the screams of seagulls. In the gloom,

Jordan's vision system picked out a warm body at the far end, near the cab. His legs cut and stinging, he tottered towards it.

The shape was a man, silenced by duct tape across his mouth. He was lying down, tied with rope to one of the upright bars, just like one of the cardboard boxes.

Jordan kneeled beside him and ripped the tape away from his mouth. "Are you Tom Flynn?" he asked.

"Yes."

Trying to undo the rope, Jordan replied, "Angel sent me."

"He's going to drive the lorry over the cliff!" Tom cried.

"What?"

"It's a protestor driving it. He'll jump out at the last second. We'll go over."

Fumbling with the rope, Jordan felt the truck braking.

Tom shouted, "Quick! We've only got a few seconds. They talked about going over this side of the old lighthouse. I tried to contact Angel but they rumbled me."

Jordan freed the last knot and yanked the rope away from his fellow agent.

They both got up and at once fell over. The sudden change of direction told them that the lorry had veered left and jumped the kerb. The vibration meant that the truck had begun to bounce across the grass towards the sheer drop over the cliff edge.

"Come on!" Jordan yelled, jumping up again and staggering down the length of the trailer to the hole at the back.

The engine snarled louder and louder. The driver was giving it full throttle to crash through the wire fence and plummet down onto the stony beach. There was a crunch as the cab barged aside a park bench.

Jordan grabbed Tom Flynn and, without wasting a second, pushed him head first out of the gap. At the same time, there was a thump and a jerk as the truck flattened two wooden fence-posts. The wires wrapped themselves around the cab but didn't stop it. The engine revved and the trailer tilted. The rear end leaped off the ground.

Jordan threw himself at the hole in the door, squeezed through, rolled down the outside and then fell through the air. He landed with a thud on the weeds right at the edge of the cliff and grabbed at a bush to steady himself.

The nervous driver had misjudged his own leap from the cab. He'd got out in time but rolled to the lip of the cliff. Unable to stop himself going over, he was now hanging on to the crumbling edge by his fingertips as the truck plunged down spectacularly, scattering the seagulls nesting on the cliff face.

The cab struck first. With a huge bang, it crumpled against the slabs of fallen rock below. The trailer landed on top of it and then fell sideways until it lay on the stones and sand like a shipwreck. Then the whole vehicle caught fire.

Flames shot up the white and red layers of rock. They singed the driver's clothes and skin. Shrieking in agony, he lost his grip on the lip of the cliff.

On impulse, Jordan thrust out his bionic arm and grabbed the man's left wrist. The driver's weight jolted Jordan forwards but he didn't topple over. He held on tightly.

Tom had been injured in the fall but he stumbled towards Jordan and lay across his blood-stained jeans, pinning his legs down and making sure he didn't tumble over the edge. He couldn't do much more.

Winter's white Audi slithered across the grass, just missed the remains of the stone arch and screeched to a halt. Winter flung the door open and rushed to the scene of the accident. Seeing both Jordan and Tom Flynn, she breathed a sigh of relief. Leaning over the edge, she looked down at the dangling driver and said, "What have we here?"

"Help!" he cried.

Winter smiled. "Jordan's only fourteen, you know."

"What?"

"He's strong but, when you're fourteen, you get tired. You can't expect him to hold you very long."

The activist spluttered and yelped like a wounded creature.

She kneeled down to get close to him. "Tell me. Did you or your group have anything to do with the Thames Estuary explosion?"

"No!" he shouted. "Get me up!"

"Why should we? What are you offering in return?"

"Please!"

Winter looked at Jordan. "Are you getting tired?"

There was something much worse than being tired. He was worried that his arm might be wrenched from its fitting to his shoulder. And his legs had gone numb. But he played her game anyway. "Very."

Winter looked down at the terrified man. "I'll tell you what. I'll check with my boss if I can do a deal with you. Hang on there a minute." She took out her phone, giggled and said, "Sorry about the pun." She hit a few buttons and then turned away, waiting for a response.

Jordan guessed that she was only pretending.

She spoke as if updating a superior on the situation

and then let out a series of responses. "Yes." "Yes." "That's right." "Okay." "I've got your go-ahead, then." "Good."

Winter squatted down again at the edge of the cliff. "Right," she said. "I can offer you a deal. If your group bombed the wreck in the Thames, you can shop the people who actually did it, and walk away free yourself. Unless Jordan drops you, of course."

"But we didn't do it! Help me." Squirming, his legs scraped against the cliff face and sent stones cascading down to the beach below.

Along with the smell of smoke, Jordan had become aware of the nearby whiff of urine. He shifted his position and his grasp of the driver's wrist slipped a little. He gripped more firmly.

A police car had turned up, but the officers had checked the registration of Winter's Audi and found it on a very special list. They would not come forward and cramp her style. They simply kept back the gathering onlookers.

"We'll even give you a new identity," Winter was saying. "We'll forget the charge of attempted murder and ship you to your country of choice. Think about it. You won't get a better trade-off. Information for your life and freedom."

"It wasn't us!"

"So, we just wait till Jordan can't hold you any more."

"Please! It really wasn't!"

Winter stared at his upturned, pleading face for at least ten seconds. "Tom," she called out, still gazing down at the panicked campaigner. "Did you hear them talking about setting off the *Richard Montgomery*?"

"No," he answered.

"See?" the activist gasped. "Nothing to do with us!"

Jordan had never before held another person's life in his hand. And it was a man who would have killed him and Tom Flynn. But Jordan refused to condemn him. He tried to remain in control. He held the driver's arm tightly enough to stop the hand slipping through his artificial fingers, but not so tightly that he cut off the man's blood supply or crushed his wrist entirely.

"You must be in touch with other political protest groups," Winter said. "Was it one of them?"

"I don't think so. Now, help me!"

Winter relented. She put her arm over the edge. "You know, I think you're telling the truth. Give me your other hand."

Together, Jordan and Winter hauled him up and onto the level ground. At once, he collapsed.

Caressing his aching shoulder with his left hand and checking that his false arm was still firmly attached, Jordan got to his feet gingerly.

Winter yelled at the police, "The driver's all yours. Is there an ambulance on its way?" Seeing the officers nod, she pointed at Tom Flynn and said, "Make sure they treat my colleague first. And when the press arrives," she added, "keep him out of it." She nodded towards her car and said to Jordan, "Come on. We've got to report to Angel. Are you all right?"

"Yeah. Sort of."

"We'll get you checked over at Highgate."

Slipping into the car, Jordan asked, "How did you know I was here?"

"It didn't take a genius. Angel was locked on to the signal from Flynn's GPS chip. He guided me in."

Jordan gazed at her as she started the engine. "Were you really going to tell me to drop that man?"

She laughed. "What do you think?"

He had just learned that she was ruthless, but he didn't want to believe that she was cold-blooded as well. "I hope not."

Making for the main road, she glanced sideways at him. "You're probably right."

Jordan sat back and wondered what would have

happened if he'd gone over the cliff in the lorry. The political campaigners would still have got publicity from their spectacular stunt, but the murder of Jordan Stryker and Tom Flynn probably would not have been splashed across the news. Tom was working undercover with a secret organization and Jordan did not officially exist. Their lives and deaths might well have passed unnoticed by everyone outside of Unit Red.

Winter sped south. For a moment, she took her eyes off the road again to look at Jordan. "More good work back there, by the way," she said. "Pity we didn't have time for a stroll along the seafront."

"It's not very nice anyway," Jordan replied wearily. "Someone's junked a lorry on the beach."

14 VANISHED

The cuts on his legs had been patched up. Apart from bruising, his shoulder had coped well with the ordeal and his mechanical arm was undamaged. A doctor and a Unit Red engineer declared him fit for duty. But the thought of continuing his mission straight away made Jordan shudder. "Do we ever get a day off?" he asked.

Winter laughed, but Angel answered, "Yep. As soon as we've caught all the bad guys, we allow ourselves a break." Then he smiled. "But you can have tomorrow to yourself. Relax a bit." He glanced down at Jordan's torn jeans and added, "Buy yourself some new trousers."

"What do I do for cash?"

"I've set up an account for you," Angel replied. "And deposited a tidy sum in it. You never asked what salary you get from Unit Red, but I don't think you'll complain. If things go well, you won't be short of funds."

In his room, Jordan glanced down at his clothes. Everything he was wearing had been provided for him by Unit Red. Jeans, shoes, jackets and all the rest had simply appeared in his cupboards. It wasn't bad gear. It wasn't embarrassing. It was the right size and shape. But it wasn't his choice. He relished the thought of going to the shops tomorrow and getting some things for himself.

He was standing in the huge window that looked over the graveyard. In the daytime, he occasionally caught sight of a distant group of visitors taking the guided tour. In the hours of darkness, the dead seemed to reclaim the cemetery. Every noise sounded sinister to Jordan. The undergrowth rustled whenever some creature stirred and the trees creaked uncannily in the wind.

His thoughts turned to the bomb blast: motives, suspects, and what he had discovered so far. He ran through every lead he had ruled out.

Melissa Pink had taken over Mr. Goss's patch, but Jordan was fairly sure that she had not marked her arrival with mass murder. Even so, if she ever got hold of him, he'd expect no mercy. He'd been caught on her territory twice, escaped twice and seen too much for his own good. He had also convinced himself that the Quickfalls and Salam Bool were not Red Devil. Mr. Bool had sought out specific people to hurt – nothing like the random violence of the Thames Estuary blast.

Like the police, Jordan didn't know if he was investigating a criminal act or terrorism, but he seemed to have eliminated anti-war, environmental, animal rights and political extremists. But he wasn't much further forward than the original enquiry. The fact that he had discovered nothing definite gnawed at him.

A fox prowled past the window. It shone yellowy-red in the infrared part of Jordan's vision. Several birds called out. Jordan recognized the sound of an owl beginning its night-time hunt.

He had the nagging feeling that everyone involved in the case of the Thames explosion was overlooking something. Or at least they hadn't asked the right questions. *He* hadn't asked the right questions. In his mind, he shut down the police file. It was no further use. He needed to think for himself. He needed to see the investigation with fresh eyes.

But right now, he needed sleep more than anything else.

Perhaps returning to Medway wasn't the best use of a day's holiday. It certainly wasn't wise when Melissa Pink's heavies were looking out for him. Yet Jordan couldn't help himself. Something drove him back. It wasn't just the shops in Strood. Thoughts of an unknown firefighter lured him back.

He hesitated outside Strood Fire Station only for a moment. Then he made for the entrance to the left of the large doors that opened in emergencies to let the fire engines out. As he entered, the man behind the desk looked at him quizzically. "Yes?" he said, clearly suspicious of a teenager. "Can I help?"

"I...erm...I'm trying to find out about one of your firemen. I mean, firefighters."

"Yes?" he repeated.

"A couple of days ago, I helped her drag someone out of a burning car in Hoo..."

The look of distrust disappeared from the fire officer's face. He leaned on the desk and nodded.

Jordan continued, "I wondered if I could have a word with her."

"I know who you mean. She told me about you. Said you were special."

Jordan hid his artificial hand by slipping it into the pocket of his new denim jacket. He shrugged. "What's her name? Is she around?"

"Debbie, we call her. Deborah Metland. And, no, she's not around. Sorry. What did you want with her?"

"She was good to me. I want to thank her."

Downcast, the fire officer sighed. Then he said, "Come outside. I need a cigarette break." He paused before adding, "Yes, I know, it's a filthy habit, especially for a fireman."

The breeze soon dispersed the trail of grey smoke from the man's nose and mouth. On the grass beside the road, hidden from it by an oversized bush, he looked into Jordan's face and said, "She's vanished."

"What?" Jordan exclaimed.

"She's not here, she's not at home, and she isn't in any of her usual haunts." He took another drag. "We've told the police. They're looking into it. But I don't think they're taking it very seriously. Not yet."

"When did she disappear?"

"Yesterday." He shook his head sadly. "Not all of the men...you know. Some of them don't think a woman's up to it. But they're wrong. Debbie's a good engineer – she works on the appliances – and a good firefighter. Remember the estuary explosion?"

Jordan nodded.

"That was her first job after basic training. Some introduction. She lost a lot, saved a few. She handled it well. Better than most." The tip of the cigarette glowed as he sucked heavily on it again.

Jordan remembered that Angel had called her a hero and a security risk. He also recalled Winter's words to the lorry driver as he dangled over the edge of Hunstanton cliff. *We'll give you a new identity and ship you to your country of choice.* Was that what had happened to Deborah Metland? Because she posed a security risk, maybe Unit Red had brushed her aside. Maybe the organization had removed her altogether.

"She was very brave," Jordan said. "That car in Hoo could have blown up when she was right by it."

"I heard she wasn't the only one," the man replied. "That's why I'm telling you all this."

* * *

Back in Highgate, Angel sat down beside the technician in the Communications Room. "Thanks for calling me. Where's he been?"

Angel and Winter had not told Jordan that he'd been fitted with a GPS chip and a microphone. They feared that Jordan would not have cooperated. They doubted that any teenager would volunteer to be under the constant surveillance of adults.

The technician tapped a few keys to access Jordan's internal tracking device. "There," he said, touching the map on the screen. "The edge of Strood. Actually, it's the fire station."

His face glum, Angel nodded. "I see. Could be important. Did you keep a record of what was said?"

"I'll send the audio file to your computer. He found out about Deborah Metland."

Angel sighed. "Where is he now?"

"Here. In the leisure park at Gillingham. He's been stationary for a few minutes."

Angel imagined his new agent looking out harmlessly over the river while, just out of his sight, police divers were searching the murky water for the remains of Salam Bool's body. "Okay," Angel said to the technician. "Keep tracking."

* * *

Jordan gazed at the Medway that led to the Thames. He was still thinking about Deborah Metland. It was very convenient for Unit Red that the firefighter had gone missing. Jordan was wondering if Angel had taken her out of the equation. If Angel had done something to her, that would make him another Salam Bool. A hitman for the good guys, but a hitman all the same.

Red Devil was also on Jordan's mind. Red Devil was always on his mind, haunting him day and night. He was desperate to find the culprit and uncover the truth behind the estuary blast.

He ran again through the events of that night twelve months earlier. He wondered who or what was the true target. Was it the people, the buildings, the businesses on and around the river, or something else? The people who had lost their lives – like Ben Smith and his family, the people in boats, those crushed by falling masonry and speared by flying glass – formed such a random group that Jordan couldn't see the sense in slaughtering them all. Maybe just one or a few of them had been the intended victims and the rest were an accidental side effect. Maybe all of the deaths were merely a by-product of hitting the real target.

Whatever the truth, Red Devil must have been utterly heartless. What grievance could possibly drive someone to such cruelty?

Of course, the destruction would not have been so overwhelming if a supertanker had not been unloading its supply of oil at Canvey Island and *Ocean Courage* had not been delivering liquefied natural gas to the terminal on the Isle of Grain when the bombs exploded. The presence of the enormous ships had been a disastrous coincidence – at least, the police teams had assumed that their presence was a coincidence.

Behind Jordan in the Strand Leisure Park, a girl screamed in frustration on the crazy-golf course, a group of boys shouted to each other in the adventure playground, and tennis balls thwacked in turn against rackets and clay.

Jordan heard all of the noises but none of them made any real impact on him. He was absorbed in a new idea. Maybe the closeness of the ships wasn't a massive coincidence at all. Maybe it was a deliberate plan.

According to all of the documents Jordan had studied, the investigators believed that Red Devil had used a time delay to allow him or her to escape before the blast. But what if that assumption had been wrong all along? What if something else dictated Red Devil's timing? What was special or important about the moment when everything went crazy? Maybe it was chosen precisely because

Ocean Courage was passing, the supertanker was unloading, or something else was happening.

Red Devil could have pressed the button before reaching a safe distance simply because he – or she – thought the river police were moving in to make an arrest. But it might have been for a different reason altogether. Maybe the target had turned up earlier than expected.

Was this the fresh thinking that the mission needed? Jordan wasn't sure. But he rushed away, eager to check it out.

Visibility in the water was almost nil. The divers could hardly see their hands in front of their faces. Each of them felt their way carefully around the bottom of the river, putting their finds in a plastic basket on a rope. Whenever they filled a basket, it was hauled up by their colleagues in a patrol boat above them. The contents were emptied onto a plastic sheet covering the deck and searched by gloved fingertips.

It was near the Upnor Road jetty that one of the officers in the boat held up two items that looked like pale twigs. He said, "I think we've got human bones here."

15 ANGRY

On its way into London, the train seemed to wait outside each station for an age before pulling up to a platform. Jordan used the time to do some more online research. He wanted to know what sort of bomb had set off the World War Two ammunition. According to police files, the forensic team had found fragments that could have come from a remote-control device or timer mechanism. There had been so little evidence left after the sequence of powerful blasts that a reliable result was impossible.

The Unit Red system did not have answers to Jordan's most important questions. Was the supertanker's cargo of oil being unloaded on schedule and was *Ocean Courage* arriving on time? At least, he couldn't find any records of shipping timetables. But he was sure that the operators of the Canvey Island oil terminal and the owners of *Ocean Courage* would have the information he needed. A simple internet search brought up a newspaper article about the wrecking of *Ocean Courage*. According to the report, it was owned by the giant power company, Energistics. Their head office was in central London.

Jordan's research was interrupted by a call from Unit Red.

"I know it's your day off," Angel's voice said, "but I thought you'd be interested in this."

"What?"

"It looks like a body got caught on one of the legs of a jetty in the river, just down from Hoo Marina. Not much flesh left, mainly bones, ligament, tendon and hair. And some bits of clothing. So it's been there a while. Maybe a year or more. I'll see if forensics can squeeze some DNA out of what the divers have brought up. That would tell us if it's Salam Bool."

"It'd be good to find out for sure," Jordan replied.

"Yes. It would bring closure."

"I could tell Vinnie Dowd. He'd be pleased to hear how it turned out."

"Where are you?"

Jordan avoided giving details. "On my way back to London," he answered. "Won't be long. Actually, I need someone to make a couple of calls about ships caught up in the big bang."

"Oh?"

"Just a minute." Jordan left his seat and went to the space at the end of the carriage. Standing on his own, he explained his latest thoughts.

"Interesting slant," said Angel. "I'll put Winter onto it."

When Jordan got back to Highgate Cemetery, he dodged round a group of tourists and tapped his code into the door lock of Unit Red's house. He didn't even make it to his room before Winter intercepted him.

Smiling at him, she announced, "You might be onto something. *Ocean Courage* was half an hour ahead of schedule when it came into the estuary."

Jordan nodded.

"There was chaos at the time. Result? The captain got no warning there was a terrorist threat in the estuary, so he just kept coming. Anyway, a ship like that's not easy to turn round or stop. It didn't have much option but to keep to its course."

Jordan hesitated for a moment and then said, "I want to go and see someone at Energistics."

"Why?" Winter asked.

"Because I've got another question."

"What's that?"

Jordan didn't want to tell her. "It might be stupid."

"Well," she said, "you'd better go and find out." She told him the company's address. "I'll call the Head of Operations again and tell him to expect you. Otherwise, they might chuck you out. Teenage troublemakers and all that."

"Okay."

"And don't mention Unit Red," she reminded him. "He thinks we're MI5. That's your cover."

Jordan turned round and headed for the door.

Winter called after him, "Hope you're having a relaxing day off."

Jordan was used to seeing the wide river estuary near Lower Stoke. From high up in Energistics' enormous building in the centre of London, the Thames was a mere strip. The boats cruising the river or moored below him in Poplar Dock Marina looked tiny.

The Head of Operations kept him waiting for nine

minutes before inviting him into a large uncluttered office. "Sit down," he said, waving towards a chair. "I was warned that you looked young, but... Anyway, what can I do for you?"

"It's about *Ocean Courage*," Jordan said. "I've seen a lot of information about it..."

"Before she was reduced to a very expensive pile of scrap metal."

"Yes," Jordan replied. "The captain was new. That's what the report said. It was his first time in charge."

"Correct," the Head of Operations confirmed. "But his inexperience wasn't the cause of the incident. It was irrelevant."

Jordan could hardly believe what he was doing. Still only fourteen, he was a Unit Red agent, halfway to the sky in a posh London office, interviewing an executive of a multinational energy company. And the time had come to ask his key question. "Why did the ship have a new captain? What happened to the old one?"

The businessman shuffled in his seat. "That's all a bit embarrassing really."

Jordan looked puzzled.

"We can't have a vessel like that – any vessel – in the hands of someone who drinks more than he should."

"So," Jordan said, "the old captain was a drunk."

"An alcoholic, yes."

"What did you do about it?"

"He gave us no choice. We sacked him."

Jordan nodded. "How did he take that?"

The Head of Operations shrugged. "Not very well. He stormed out."

"He was angry?"

"Absolutely."

"Did he say anything?" Jordan asked.

"Not to me. He muttered something to himself, though."

"What?"

"I didn't catch it. A threat, probably. I imagine most of his words were not for the faint-hearted."

"A threat?"

"Probably," he repeated.

"So," Jordan said, "he might have threatened to get his own back on you, the company, the workers – or the ship."

The Head of Operations sat bolt upright. "I didn't think anything of it. We all get angry and issue threats. We don't follow them up once we've cooled off." He gazed at Jordan for a moment and then asked, "Are you implying...?" He didn't finish his question.

"I don't know if he's got anything to do with the

explosion," Jordan replied, "but you'd better tell me who he was."

The company executive took a deep breath. "I can't reveal personal details of employees – or ex-employees – but, under the circumstances... His name was Captain Norman Lightfoot."

"Norman Lightfoot," Jordan said excitedly.

"Who's Norman Lightfoot?" Angel asked.

"He's in charge of Chalkwell Marina where Cara Quickfall kept her boat. I went there when I was in Southend. I was trying to find out who'd used it."

"So you met him?" said Winter.

"Yes. I pretended I was after a job."

Angel and Winter glanced at each other. "Well, let's hope you didn't scare him off." Angel's tone wasn't critical. He was simply stating a fact.

Jordan defended himself anyway. "I didn't know who he was then."

"I realize that," Angel replied. It took only a second for him to decide Unit Red's next move. "I want both of you to go to Southend and find him. He'd got a motive – revenge – and easy access to Cara Quickfall's boat. Let's see if he ticks any more boxes. I'll find out where he lives and dig out his background while you're on your way. It'll take for ever to drive out of London and along the A13. So, take the Tube to London Bridge and agree a strategy between you on the way. I'll have a speedboat waiting for you by the time you get there. Use the river."

Jordan stood next to Winter, gripping the canopy, and wondered if there was anything she couldn't drive. She'd jumped into the motorboat and taken off without hesitation. She was guiding it expertly round the twists and turns of the Thames, weaving eastwards through London. Perhaps she could fly helicopters and planes as well.

Jordan also noticed that she was carrying a gun inside her coat.

As they passed City Airport, Jordan's mobile vibrated in his pocket. He concentrated on listening to Angel's voice over the noise of the wind and the outboard motor.

"Norman Lightfoot ticks *all* the boxes. He was a strong swimmer, according to his school reports. That means he could have survived when the estuary erupted – if it was him in the Quickfalls' boat. And his first job was in the navy. He was a diver and he dealt with underwater explosives." Angel dictated Lightfoot's address and then added, "I'll get back to you if I find out anything else significant."

Raising his voice, Jordan told Winter what Angel had discovered.

She nodded. "I think we've got our first credible suspect. And we only need one – if it's the right one."

While they powered past Gravesend, Angel phoned with yet more news. "The man who owns Chalkwell Marina isn't happy. He's had to hire someone else to do Lightfoot's job because he hasn't shown up for work since Tuesday last week. No explanation. You saw him that evening so it looks like you *did* scare him off. Just one more thing. He's never been married. There isn't a wife, known partner or children. That's all I've got. It's over to you and Winter."

The sun had gone down somewhere behind London, but the river was never truly dark. The lights on either side allowed Winter to see exactly where she was going. Gate-crashing the moorings next to Southend's funfair, she tied up the boat, strode onto Western Esplanade and hailed a cab.

Jordan gave Norman Lightfoot's address in Rochford to the driver and sat back. He tried to look as relaxed as Winter, but he didn't manage it.

They jumped out as soon as the taxi came to a halt outside the unlit house at the edge of Southend-on-Sea. Opening the gate, they walked up to the front door and Winter pounded on the brass knocker.

There was no answer.

After a second try, she said, "We'll attract less attention at the back door."

Following her round the side of the upmarket house, Jordan asked, "What are we going to do now?"

"We're going in," she answered. "We haven't got permission, but it's urgent and important, don't you think?"

Jordan nodded in the darkness. "Sure."

"So," Winter said, pointing at the door, "let us in."

Luckily, there was nothing behind the house apart from a long garden and a golf course. The trees to either side protected them from prying neighbours.

"What if it's got a burglar alarm?"

"There wasn't an alarm box at the front, so I'm willing to bet it hasn't got one. If I'm wrong, I'll get Angel to hold the police off."

"Okay." Jordan breathed in, steeled himself and crashed through the door.

16 BLUFF

There was an unearthly silence after Jordan had wrenched the door from its lock. They both crept into the darkened house.

"I can't see much," Winter complained. "Use your night vision to find all the downstairs windows and close the curtains. Then we'll risk turning the lights on and have a look around."

The air was stale. Jordan felt uncomfortable padding around someone else's home, but he was surprised to feel a shiver of excitement at the thought of doing something unlawful.

Once he'd pulled the curtains across every downstairs window, he turned on the hall lights. Straight away, Winter bent down and grabbed the handful of letters scattered on the carpet by the front door. Peering at the postmarks, she said, "He hasn't picked up his mail for at least a week." She dropped the envelopes and instead put Lightfoot's phone to her ear for a few seconds. "No messages," she whispered. "Come on. Let's get on with it. A diary would be great, but I'd settle for a computer."

In the living room, the first thing to catch Jordan's eye was a framed photo of Norman Lightfoot in uniform standing on the bridge of *Ocean Courage*. He held it up for Winter to see.

She nodded. "That's where you'd expect to see a picture of him and his wife. He was married to his ship." Noticing some photo albums on the bookshelf, she took the most prominent one and flicked through it.

Jordan stood beside her as she looked at pages and pages of Norman Lightfoot in exotic locations. Each shot had a neatly handwritten caption.

"I suppose that's what happens when you're a sea captain," she said. "You get around. He took a lot of pictures in Norway. Trondheim in particular. I guess that's because of the North Sea oil industry – or maybe he takes holidays there."

She replaced the album on the shelf, walked past the well-stocked drinks' cabinet and went back into the hall.

Jordan pointed to a door on the left. He'd seen enough with his infrared vision to know what it was. "That's a study," he told her.

"Good." She went in and felt around the wall until she found the light switch. Turning it on, she said, "Ah. Here we go. You get into the computer, Jordan. I'm going to go through the desk and paperwork."

About to press the computer's on/off button with his left hand, he hesitated. "Does it matter about fingerprints?"

"Use your right hand if you want to avoid it, but don't worry too much. Didn't I cover this in briefings? Your fingerprints – and mine – are in a special file. If the police come across them, they won't ask questions." For a moment, she stopped flicking through pieces of paper. "They leave us alone because they know we'll give them the bad guy on a plate, melt away, and let them take the credit."

The monitor came to life in front of Jordan and he groaned. "It's protected by a password."

"Don't let a little thing like that put you off. Take a guess."

He sighed and then typed *password*, but the system did not let him in. *NormanLightfoot* didn't work either. But his third guess, *OceanCourage*, opened the door. "I'm in," he said, his voice a little too loud. "It wasn't the world's cleverest password."

Jordan clicked on *My Documents* and at once he had a list of folders and files. Immediately, he was drawn towards Norman Lightfoot's C.V. It was a year old and it had been prepared to apply for the job in Chalkwell Marina. Jordan skimmed through the document. "It's all here. Just like Angel said. Years in the navy, an experienced diver and strong swimmer. He's good at a lot of modern foreign languages. Fluent in Norwegian."

"Keep looking," Winter replied. "What else is there? Any e-mails?"

Jordan started the e-mail package and then nodded. "Yes. He sent his last one on 11th April – the day after I went to the boatyard." He opened the most recent messages that Norman had written. "There's nothing interesting. Hang on. I'll do a search on the whole computer."

But he drew a blank.

Jordan also searched all documents for the terms

Richard Montgomery and *explosive*, with the same result. Lightfoot had no files containing those giveaway words.

"I'm going into Internet Explorer." Jordan clicked on *History* to see the websites that Lightfoot had visited before he disappeared. He scanned down the sites and then gasped.

"What is it?"

"He did a search on my name. *Jordan Stryker*."

"You *did* spook him last week," Winter said. "But it's okay. He won't have discovered anything about you."

Feeling unsettled, Jordan continued down the list. "Look," he said. "This might be important. Websites about shipping."

Together they went through the pages he'd visited. The last time Norman Lightfoot had logged on to the internet, he'd delved into the schedules and destinations of ships leaving the Thames Estuary. His final piece of research concerned a ship leaving for Trondheim in Norway.

Winter smiled. "I'm getting a consistent message here. It doesn't take a genius to work out where he's gone. Let's face it: he'd be expert at getting out of the country by ship. He's bound to know how to sneak on board without raising suspicions." She put down a notepad and said, "He hasn't left a trail on paper. Come on. Best to get out of here before the cops arrive. I think our work's done."

"But we haven't proved anything..."

"No, but the innocent don't do a runner when a boy comes sniffing around," Winter replied. "Anyway, we know where to find him. I'll settle for that."

"All right," Angel said to Winter. "I'll book you onto a flight for Trondheim tonight – if there is one. And I'll have a team go with you. Well, a couple of agents. That's all I can spare. But it's enough."

Winter nodded.

Jordan looked at Angel with expectation on his face.

Angel shook his head. "You lost your holiday today. You can have tomorrow off instead."

"But..." Jordan began.

"No, Jordan. You've been really helpful, I know, but you're not going. That's final. Think about it. Unit Red doesn't exist. We don't have any authority in Norway. Winter and the others will go as tourists. You'd be a minor travelling without parents. That'd raise too many tricky questions with immigration officials."

"And getting you through the metal detector would take some explaining," Winter said with a grin.

"That's not all," Angel added. "Lightfoot would make a run for it if he saw you coming."

Angel's decision was as solid as a brick wall that even Jordan's arm could not demolish. There was no point even trying.

Lying in bed that night, though, doubts began to niggle at Jordan, keeping sleep away. He wondered if Angel and Winter had jumped to the obvious conclusion too quickly. What if Norman Lightfoot had laid a false trail – all the way to Norway? What if he'd anticipated that the powers-that-be would find all of the information in his house? What if it was a deliberate bluff? After all, the pictures of Norway had been left lying around, his computer password had been easy to crack, and he hadn't deleted the record of his internet search history.

Maybe that was too far-fetched. Maybe the disgraced captain had thought about leaving the country – and even researched it on the internet – but decided it was an over-the-top reaction to a boy asking questions. As far as Norman Lightfoot knew, he was up against a curious teenager. He didn't know he had Unit Red on his scent. He could be in a clinic dealing with his drink problem. He could be anywhere sorting his head out. He could be on a massive drunken binge. Or he could still be in Chalkwell.

Jordan realized what he had to do. Tomorrow he would sacrifice another day's holiday and return to the marina where he'd met Norman Lightfoot, where Cara Quickfall used to moor her boat.

17 TRAP

Jordan walked back along the seaside lane towards Chalkwell Marina. On his left, beyond the sandbank, a tanker entering the mouth of the Thames seemed to be moving at walking pace in the same direction. Going much faster, a train bound for London rumbled past him on the right. He hadn't got a plan in mind. He just knew he had to go to the boatyard and check it out for clues on Lightfoot's whereabouts.

He hesitated at the corner of the marina and looked

down on the landing stage. It contained the same range of boats: from cheap to costly, from shoddy to smart. Three of the moorings were empty.

It struck Jordan that looking after a few family boats would be quite a comedown for the sacked captain of *Ocean Courage*. After being in charge of a giant ship, every day working in this small marina would remind him of his fall from favour. Every day, he would feel humiliated. But was that enough of a motive to kill so many people? If Norman Lightfoot had sabotaged the *Richard Montgomery*, maybe he'd expected the effects to be limited to the passing *Ocean Courage*. That's where his real grievance lay. Maybe he hadn't meant to cause such a massive catastrophe.

No one seemed to be around. The door to the shack was closed. Wondering what he'd do if Lightfoot was hiding inside, Jordan breathed in the clean sea air and went towards the familiar shed.

Readying his robotic arm for action, he banged on the door with his left hand and opened it without waiting for an answer. But no one rushed at him.

A young man jumped up from the chair by the computer as if taken by surprise. "Hello?" he said.

The walls were still covered with the same pictures, but the smell of whisky had gone. Jordan was both relieved and disappointed. Trying to act naturally, he grinned. "Computer games instead of logging boats, eh?"

"Who are you?"

"I could ask you that. Norman knows me. He looked after my mum's boat. Cara Quickfall. Is he around?"

The new manager checked the boatyard's spreadsheet and found a reference to the Quickfall family. He seemed to relax, believing that Jordan was genuine. "I took over a week back. Mr. Lightfoot left. I don't know why."

"That's a shame," Jordan replied. It meant that the discharged captain really had vanished. "I wanted him to help me sort out what to do about our boat. It went missing ages ago."

"Yours too?" he blurted out.

"What do you mean? Has another one been nicked?"

"No, I don't suppose so. It was Mr. Lightfoot's and it's gone." He brought up the details on the monitor. "I guess he took off in it."

Jordan edged towards the computer screen. "Can I see?"

The young man stood in front of the monitor. "Why?"

With a grin on his face, Jordan replied, "Because I'm part of a secret organization investigating Norman Lightfoot."

The man laughed. "Yeah. Right. Nice line."

Jordan said, "If I know which boat was his, it'll help me find him."

The manager stood aside. "I'll let you look if you don't tell anyone."

"Done." Jordan bent closer to the screen. "*Windsong*. A lot posher than ours. And it was last logged on Tuesday 17th April."

"Yes," he said. "Before I started."

Jordan nodded. "Interesting."

Jordan stood on the triangle of sandy beach outside Chalkwell Station and watched some kids messing about at the edge of the water. "It might look like he's gone to Norway," Jordan explained to Angel, "but I think he's really living in a boat called *Windsong*. All one word. We need to check for sightings. It's a Sealine S28 Bolero sports cruiser, made in 1998. I don't know what half of that means, but I memorized it from the spreadsheet."

"I'm not convinced Winter's on a wild goose chase," Angel said into his ear. "Perhaps Lightfoot expected you to go back to Chalkwell so he hid his boat, knowing you'd come to the wrong conclusion. I think it's more likely you've sniffed out the decoy and Winter's onto the real thing."

Jordan's mood took a tumble. He hadn't thought of that.

"But I'll put someone onto it anyway. You sunbathe – or whatever you want to do with your day off by the seaside – and I'll call you back if we get any hits."

Jordan was sitting on the seawall and drinking Coke when his phone rang again.

It was Angel. "Get yourself a taxi to Burnham-on-Crouch. It's just round the corner from where you are. About forty kilometres by road."

"Why?" Jordan asked.

"Because *Windsong*'s moored there, according to the local authorities. Along with hundreds of yachts. But you'll find it if you look hard enough. And Jordan?"

"Yes?"

"Take care. Just in case Lightfoot is there."

The Crouch was dotted with countless buoys and boats. Their masts cluttered the skyline like exclamation marks. Yachting clubs sent lines of pontoons into the river and, further out, colourful sails ballooned in the wind.

Burnham-on-Crouch seemed to exist for sailing. It had the laid-back atmosphere of a model village, as if it wasn't part of the real world. The Quay was buzzing even though it was Friday and not a weekend. It wasn't even in the tourist season. Perhaps there was going to be a yachting event of some sort.

Jordan had his vision on maximum as he walked slowly beside the river, trying to spot one particular boat among the many. He grumbled into his phone, "Can't they pin it down a bit more? 'Not in one of the marinas' means anywhere in the river. And that's overflowing with yachts."

"What you're after should stand out," Angel replied. "It's a powerboat. It doesn't have a mast. It's a white sporty number with a rail around the front. If you want to see what it looks like, I've put a photo on the system."

"I'll check it out, but everything I'm seeing here is a yacht or a rowing boat."

He dodged around a group of people drinking beer outside a hotel and almost tripped over a dog lead. He continued along the front, straining to see as far as possible across the wide waterway. Along the front, there were no amusement arcades or other trappings of the tourist trade. The River Crouch was Burnham's attraction.

He was just coming up to a series of landing stages for larger boats when he saw it. At least, he saw something that matched Angel's description. He was too far away to see the motorboat's name. He stopped and concentrated. In his mind, he compared the profile with the picture on Unit Red's computer. And it matched.

Looking round to make sure no one was watching him, he ran out along a jetty and scrambled down two wooden steps into a dinghy. He untied it and began to row out into the river towards the white sports cruiser. He was clumsy. He had not done much rowing and his right arm was so much stronger than his left that it threatened to drive him round in circles. He reduced power to his artificial arm to try and make it match his real one. After a few minutes he began to get the hang of it. He wove his way between yachts tied to buoys.

As he drew closer to the powerboat, he could see that he'd got the right vessel. The name, *Windsong*, was painted in handwriting style near the prow. There was no one on deck.

Jordan found it difficult to manoeuvre the dinghy up to the motorboat's stern where there was a step for boarding. One of the oars kept getting in the way. In the end, he pulled as hard as he could on both oars, propelling himself in the right direction, and then removed the oars from their rowlocks while the dinghy glided up to *Windsong*. He reached out and grabbed the rear of the powerboat and stood up, ready to step across, but the dinghy went backwards and he toppled.

He splashed down into the cold river. His sodden clothes and heavy arm dragged him down further than he expected. Underwater, he could see a grid of orange mooring ropes and something attached to the bottom of *Windsong*. He wasn't an expert on boats but he knew that a box about the size of a small suitcase did not belong there.

He broke the surface, took a gulp of air and dived down again. Swimming up to the metal object, he couldn't figure out what it was, but it certainly wasn't part of the design. It had been attached with suction pads.

Then it dawned on him. He could be looking at the same type of explosive device that had been attached to the *Richard Montgomery*. *Windsong* had been booby-trapped. He guessed that the bomb had been rigged to blow if he went on board or if Lightfoot, watching from a distance with a remote control, saw him clamber on deck.

The boat could be both a test and a trap. Norman Lightfoot could well have set it up to check if Jordan was hunting him and, if he was, to put an end to that hunt.

Jordan knew he had to get away.

Chilled, he rose to the surface and swam a few strokes

to the dinghy. Almost capsizing the boat, he yanked himself awkwardly up and into it at the third attempt. He brushed wet hair from his face, refitted the oars and rowed away as quickly as he could, driving the dinghy back to the shore.

He tied the boat hurriedly to the jetty and pulled himself up onto the wooden platform. Dripping water from his saturated clothes, he shivered and surveyed the riverside walkway. He couldn't see Norman Lightfoot, but there were too many people around to be certain he wasn't there. Jordan expected him to be nearby, keeping an eye on his trap.

A toddler pointed at Jordan and giggled. "That boy's all wet!"

Jordan realized for the first time that a few people were staring at him. He shrugged and hurried back down The Quay, looking frantically around. Sidestepping the prams and pushchairs, dogs, slow-moving old folk and small groups of people who had stopped for a chat, Jordan continued along the promenade. As he went, he warmed up and forgot how uncomfortable he felt.

He left The Quay and headed towards the Royal Corinthian Yacht Club that jutted out over the water. Four yachts were perched on the decking. And Norman Lightfoot was sitting out on the veranda.

Jordan came to a sudden halt and gasped. His main suspect was just sitting there, not paying much attention to anything except the glass and bottle on the table in front of him. No wonder he hadn't spotted Jordan rowing out to *Windsong* in the distance. He was probably drunk.

Straight away, Jordan decided to confront Lightfoot. He didn't know the building, but it looked like he'd have to go round to the main door and through the club to reach the balcony. But as he set off, he thought the old sea captain might have glanced in his direction. If he was right, he had to hope that Lightfoot hadn't recognized him among the swarm of yachting enthusiasts.

Jordan burst into the club through the roadside entrance and dashed to the waterside balcony, leaving startled sailors in his wake. He skidded to a halt on the veranda. But Norman Lightfoot was no longer there. Only an empty bottle, a pair of binoculars and an ashtray containing the butt of a cigar remained on his table. Jordan sighed heavily and walked to the railing at the edge of the balcony. He hung over it but could not see anyone retreating from the club.

Frustrated, he drummed his fingers on the top rail. He hadn't dried off completely but he'd stopped dripping so at least he was attracting less attention. The few people relaxing on the veranda ignored him.

Jordan could make out the distant *Windsong*. Then he became aware of something else. His heightened sense of smell picked up a familiar scent. It was a mixture of alcohol and cigars. It wasn't coming from the table. It was very close. Jordan spun round.

Lightfoot had sneaked up behind him and in his hand was his broken tumbler. He thrust the jagged glass at Jordan, aiming at his neck.

18 BROKEN

Instinctively, Jordan dodged out of the way and let fly with his right arm. It slammed into Lightfoot's chest, glanced off and cracked against his chin. The broken glass flew across the floor and the blow lifted Norman off his feet, even though he was big and solid. He jolted backwards and crumpled onto the floor.

A group of bar staff, bouncers and club members burst out onto the balcony and came at Jordan. Before he could react, they had him by the arms. He didn't strike out again. Shocked by his own power, he didn't want to hurt anyone else. A yachtsman helped Norman Lightfoot up and supported him as he walked away.

"No!" Jordan cried. "You've got it wrong. I'm the good guy. He attacked me."

"Sure," one of the men replied. "Fifty-year-old attacks teenager. That's a turn-up for the books."

"How come he's hurt if he's the thug?" someone said.

"We've called the police."

Jordan shouted, "You didn't see. You don't understand!"

"Save it for the police."

"Till they come, you're under citizens' arrest."

"Why don't we get some rope and tie him up?"

A girl – about seven or eight years old – walked towards them timidly and said in a quiet voice, "He's telling the truth. The bad man tried to hurt him."

A woman – the girl's mother, Jordan assumed – kneeled down beside her. "Are you sure, Sophie? What did you see?"

Sophie pointed to the steps that led down to the pontoon and the area underneath the balcony. "The man was hiding down there. He came up all quiet. On tiptoe, you know." She demonstrated a few silent steps. "He was holding a broken glass. He tried to stab..." She looked at Jordan and then fell silent.

Suddenly embarrassed, the men let go of Jordan.

Jordan nodded at Sophie and then said to the men, "I'm on the same side as the police. And I'm pretty sure the man you've just let off blew up the Thames Estuary. I think he's put a bomb in the river here as well."

"What? Here? A bomb?"

The chief barman rushed to the door and shouted inside, "Don't let him go!"

But it was too late. Norman Lightfoot had got his breath back and staggered out of the club.

The background noise was almost deafening as club members asked questions, wondering what was going on. Jordan was at the centre of the fuss, yet a distant cry made him suddenly alert. "Hey! That's mine. Come back!" At once, he shouldered his way through the crowd and looked over the rail.

Lightfoot was sailing away in a tiny yacht, while its owner stood at the end of the jetty waving his arms furiously and shouting.

Jordan squatted down briefly by the girl and said, "Thanks, Sophie. I've got to go and catch him."

"Okay," she replied.

He stood up and dashed to the steps that were out of

sight around the corner of the balcony. He went down them two at a time, almost out of control. He sprinted towards the yachtsman at the end of the pontoon. Both of them watched Norman Lightfoot meandering clumsily under a brilliant orange sail. "I don't know anything about yachts," Jordan said to him, "but you do. So, let's grab someone else's and go after him."

The man stared at Jordan for a few seconds and then seemed to click into action. "Yes. Of course. Harry will understand. We'll take his." He hurried along the jetty to another yacht and Jordan followed him.

Unfurling the mainsail and jib, the yachtsman muttered angrily, "That idiot doesn't know about sailing either. He's all over the place. Not in control at all. If he damages my boat, I'll murder him."

Jordan smiled. "I'll help."

The wind caught the sail and the yacht lurched away from the jetty. "Do you know him?" the sailor asked. "Keep down, by the way."

Jordan ducked as the boom flew across and threatened to remove his head. "Yes. He's used to something a bit bigger than yachts. When you catch him up, let me handle him. He's dangerous."

"Fine. You take care of him. I'll take care of the boats." Keeping his eye on the river, the man paused and then said, "I'm Charles. Who are you?"

"Jordan."

"Good to meet you," he said, his tone heavily ironic.

The red and white sail swelled and strained above them. The hull sliced through the water and the whole yacht tilted. Jordan felt as if he was taking a corner on a speeding motorbike. They accelerated westwards.

"The key is to angle the sail," Charles said as he adjusted the jibsheet. Then he gazed ahead. "That chap hasn't got a clue. I just hope we get to him before he collides with something."

Still keeping his head down, Jordan pointed to a large motorboat coming across the river. "Talking of collisions..."

"It's the Wallasea ferry. I've got it covered."

"I didn't mean you," Jordan replied.

Norman Lightfoot's yacht appeared to Jordan to be swerving into the path of the ferry.

Charles muttered, "The fool!"

Making for its landing stage in Burnham, the ferry sounded its foghorn as a warning.

Jordan could just see Lightfoot. He seemed confused by ropes, tiller and sails. It was likely that panic and alcohol were adding to his confusion. His yacht veered crazily, the boom swung across and struck the incompetent sailor across the head. He collapsed at once. The boat turned away from the approaching ferry and instead headed for the northern shore. Without anyone to steer, though, it was bound to ram one of the moored boats before it reached land.

In the distance, a police siren wailed.

Concentrating on the stolen yacht with the bright orange sail, Jordan realized where it was going. Straight towards *Windsong*. He turned towards Charles and said, "Don't go any closer!"

"What? Why not? I've got to intercept it."

"No!" Jordan yelled at him. "There's a bomb."

"A what?"

"Over there. Where it's going. If it hits..."

"What do you mean? What about my boat?"

"Look," Jordan said. "Phew! It's okay. It's going to miss."

But Charles's hijacked yacht glanced off one moored vessel, changed direction and headed directly towards *Windsong*.

Jordan closed his eyes, winced, and braced himself. He saw a huge column of water and bright flashes. He heard a massive explosion followed by a series of thunderous bangs. He saw a window shatter in front of him. He saw glass piercing his body as he was blown backwards. And he saw his right arm wrenched from his shoulder. But he felt...nothing.

He opened his eyes. The yacht had slammed into *Windsong* but there had been no explosion. No injuries. No damage. Nothing. His imagination – and his fear – had transported him back in time to a year earlier.

Charles was still manoeuvring the borrowed boat closer to his own.

A groggy Norman Lightfoot had scrambled onto *Windsong* and he was tottering around. Blood was leaking from his head wound and alcohol probably clouded his mind. He hadn't even noticed Jordan. He yanked on the door to the living quarters, but he couldn't open it. Stumbling around the deck, he could barely keep upright. He searched one pocket after another until he came across the key. In trying to push it into the lock, he dropped it and cursed.

Jordan's companion was interested only in the yacht that had begun to drift at the whim of wind and tide. He fought heroically with rudder, ropes and sail, trying to get alongside.

Giving up with the key and opting for brute force, Lightfoot battered the door until it gave way. And that was the trigger.

The bomb attached to the keel detonated.

The blast was nowhere near as dramatic as the one in the Thames Estuary, but the powerboat's fuel exploded. Parts of *Windsong* flew apart and the rest caught fire. Water erupted and Norman Lightfoot was tossed into the air along with the fibreglass shrapnel from the devastated boat. The force of the blast snapped the mast of Charles's unmanned yacht and shredded its orange sail. Fragments of nylon fell from the sky like burst balloons. The boat itself flipped over. Its centreboard and rudder poked up out of the water like sharks' fins.

Jordan felt the heat on his face and he gripped the side of the boat as it rocked uncontrollably from side to side.

"What the...!" Charles hung on to the mainsheet with his mouth open.

"Over there!" Jordan called out, pointing at Norman Lightfoot's body. He was floating face down on the water.

Charles guided the yacht through the flotsam. Jordan leaned over the side and grabbed Lightfoot's arm. The old sea captain's body was incredibly heavy but Jordan steeled himself and began to heave him onboard with his powerful right arm. Behind Jordan, Charles leaned over the opposite side to counterbalance Norman's weight and to stop the yacht capsizing.

Jordan landed his catch. Norman Lightfoot flopped into the yacht like a wounded whale and Jordan said, "Let's get him to land."

"Is he dead?"

Jordan shrugged.

Lightfoot was a dreadful sight. Much of his skin was burned, his left leg was missing below the knee and watery blood was streaming from the wound. But both of his eyes remained stubbornly open.

Was this shattered man responsible for killing Ben Smith, his family and so many others? Jordan was already sure. He leaned over Norman Lightfoot. "You're not dead, are you?" he said. "I don't know if you can hear me, but you'll survive. If I could, you will as well. And you know what? I'm glad. I want you to pull through. I want you to live with it."

19 PROOF

The Crouch Harbour Authority and the police were waiting at the jetty. Jordan did not need to explain who he was because a mystery man, sent by Angel, had already spoken to them. He didn't know how the agent had worked out exactly where he was, but he was very grateful for the backup. While an ambulance raced to the scene and a first-aider tightened a tourniquet round the remains of Lightfoot's left leg, Jordan simply told the police what had happened and Charles nodded his agreement absent-mindedly.

A few minutes later, the ambulance took the disgraced captain to the nearest hospital with a police escort. Angel's assistant whisked Jordan away in a Jaguar. Along with the harbour master, Charles was left standing on the jetty, staring glumly at the river and the remains of his precious yacht.

On the way back to London, Jordan sat in silence. He had imagined how this moment would feel. He'd expected to run around and punch the air as if he'd just scored the winning goal. But he didn't feel like it. He wasn't ready to celebrate. He wasn't content. He wanted to believe he'd discovered Red Devil and handed him over to the police. He wanted to believe he'd succeeded where everyone else had failed. But where was the proof that he'd completed his mission?

Norman Lightfoot would not be convicted because he looked guilty; because he ticked all the boxes, as Angel put it. Unit Red's job was to prove a case against the bad guys. To make this one watertight, Jordan felt he needed more evidence. He wished there was a way to detect Lightfoot's fingerprints all over the crime. But Jordan wasn't a forensic scientist and the original crime scene had been obliterated twelve months earlier.

Desperate for proof, Jordan wondered why the man

who'd once captained *Ocean Courage* had walked into his own booby trap on board *Windsong*. Lightfoot could have been dazed, drunk or depressed. So depressed by what he had done that he wanted to blow himself up. If that was true, perhaps his attempt at suicide was an admission of guilt.

Something else stopped Jordan celebrating. The arrest hadn't changed anything. The disaster had still happened and it could never be undone. His family was still dead and, as Jordan Stryker, he still had to remain a stranger to Amy Goss.

The next day, as Jordan sat in the bunker, he wondered if the dead of Highgate Cemetery were also curious and eager to hear Angel's words. He could picture them pressing their decomposing ears against the other side of the wall.

Angel stopped typing and turned towards his young recruit. "You look like you're in a world of your own."

"Just thinking," Jordan replied.

"What about?"

He jerked his thumb at the wall behind Angel. "The graveyard."

Angel nodded. "It's because of the dead that I asked

you to come down. We've got some loose ends to tie up."

"Oh?"

Angel glanced at his computer screen. "Those remains we pulled out of the river near Hoo Marina. The DNA was degraded, but there was enough to be sure we've seen the last of Salam Bool. End of that part of the story."

Jordan didn't feel sympathy, only relief. "I'll let Vinnie Dowd know."

"I guess we owe him that."

"Is that all?" asked Jordan.

"No."

"Is it Norman Lightfoot? He hasn't died, has he?"

Angel shook his head. "No. He's under sedation in hospital."

"What then?"

"I'm not satisfied he'll be convicted. If he gets a good lawyer... We don't really have the killer piece of evidence. It's all circumstantial."

"Unless he admits he did it," said Jordan.

Angel nodded. "That'd help, but I'd still like to see solid evidence."

"I want to go and talk to him."

"What?" Angel looked troubled.

"I want to hear him confess. You could record it if you fitted me with a hidden microphone or something."

For an instant, Angel looked surprised. Then he put up his palm. "I'm not convinced. I don't know how you'll react when you come face-to-face with him. Revenge is a powerful emotion."

Jordan realized that Angel's decision was final. It was a waste of time arguing. He stared at the floor for a few seconds and then looked up. "I know."

"What?"

"How to get evidence," Jordan said excitedly. "If you get bits of bomb from the Crouch explosion and compare them with those fragments left over after the estuary blast..." He looked at Angel and said, "Why are you smiling like that?"

"Because you're on the ball. I've already got forensics working on it."

"There's another thing. I bet he was going to set it off with some sort of remote. If they find that, it might match what he used on the *Richard Montgomery*."

"Good point." Angel typed something into his laptop and then stood up. "Look, you deserve that break you keep missing. I'll probably get the results on Tuesday. Till then, you're on leave."

* * *

Over the weekend, Winter returned empty-handed from Norway and Jordan phoned Vinnie Dowd to tell him what had happened to Salam Bool. But Jordan believed someone else deserved to know. After all, Amy Goss had given him the lead he needed to discover the truth. He set out to meet her after school on Monday, but he didn't announce his intentions to Angel, Winter or anyone else in Unit Red.

He lurked for a while outside Amy's school but felt too exposed there. Worried that one of Melissa Pink's thugs might walk or drive past and notice him, he moved on. He went down Main Road, crossed over, and took the quiet lane that Amy used to walk home. Less conspicuous, but unaware that he'd already been spotted, he sat on a wall and waited.

He couldn't go to Amy's house and linger there because Jordan Stryker would not know where she lived. She'd be very suspicious if she thought he'd somehow managed to find her address. Then there was Mr. Goss. If Amy's dad saw him outside their house, he might send out some heavies – if he still had any.

Yet, after twenty minutes, there was no sign of her.

Jordan decided to take a gamble. Reckoning that there was one place she might have gone, he set out for the farm in Lower Stoke. He was so intent on finding her that he forgot to make sure no one was watching and following him.

As he squeezed between the grain silos, a voice said, "Hey? Mr. Bool's creepy but heroic next-door neighbour."

Jordan was delighted to find her, even if she'd reminded him straight away of the lie he'd told her last time they'd met. He looked at her and said, "Sort of."

Actually, more than one lie had come between them. He'd put his injuries down to a car crash and he'd given her a false name. Outside of Unit Red, though, the only person to figure out who he really was had disappeared. Jordan believed he was working for the good guys, but he wondered if Unit Red had blown away the firefighter who had saved his life. He didn't want Amy to suffer the same fate so he had to keep her in the dark for her own protection.

"Why are you here? Been thrown out of the sports club again?"

"No. I was looking for you." He smiled and sat down on the cold ground. "I just thought you'd want to know what I found out about Mr. Bool."

"And you guessed I'd be here?"

"I missed you outside school and I couldn't think of anywhere else to try."

Amy nodded as if she almost believed him – but not quite. "So, what's with Mr. Bool?"

"He's dead. Ed Hathaway killed him. Not on purpose. Not really. They had a bit of a scrap and Mr. Bool banged his head. That's why Ed went away."

Amy looked puzzled. "Why didn't anyone say anything?"

"No one knew," Jordan answered. "Ed and his mates pushed him out in a boat and it sank. His body was trapped underwater. The police have just found it."

Somewhere nearby, the engines of farm vehicles spluttered into life. Jordan turned down his hearing.

"Well," Amy said, "I didn't like him, but..."

Jordan shook his head. "Don't feel too sorry for him. Do you want to know what he did for a living?"

"Teach?"

"Apart from that. He had a nasty sideline."

"You're weird," Amy said abruptly. "It's like you know too much. Like you're a cop or something."

Jordan shrugged. "I just asked a few questions. Got a few answers. That's all." He hoped that the real parts of his cheeks had not turned bright red.

"Okay. What's his other job, Sherlock? You're itching to tell me."

"He beat people up to get money out of them."

"What?" Amy cried out.

"It's a long story." Deciding where to begin, Jordan drummed his fingers on one of the metal struts. He took a deep breath, took one look at Amy and stopped before he started.

Amy was staring at him, her face completely drained of colour.

"What is it?"

She could barely speak. She raised a hand and pointed at him. "I know who you are! Not Jordan at all!"

It was Jordan's turn to gasp in astonishment. "What do you mean?"

She scrambled to her feet and nodded towards his left hand, still resting on the silo. "There's only one person who does that."

"What?"

"Taps a rhythm out like that. No one does it as well as..." She still looked startled, her eyes wide open. And she was breathing rapidly. "You're..."

They both jolted as a tractor rammed into the gap between the silos. On the opposite side, two more farm machines crashed into the metal containers and blocked off their retreat.

Melissa Pink and her bodyguards clambered over the

wreckage, violating the secret meeting place. More heavies stood outside, encircling the area.

They were trapped. Instinctively, Jordan and Amy moved together in the centre of the space.

"What do we have here?" Melissa said with glee all over her freckled face. "Goss's daughter if I'm not mistaken." Shorter than both of them, she didn't risk getting too close. She smiled at Jordan and said, "Confirmation, I think, that you work for Goss. Maybe you're young Amy's minder."

"Wrong," Amy said. "He doesn't work for my dad."

Amy must have known she was facing her dad's victorious rival because she almost spat.

Melissa was plainly enjoying another moment of triumph over the Goss family, enjoying her power. "So, what's going on here? Is it a love nest? How sweet. And quite a catch for me. Must be my lucky day."

Amy growled, "My dad will..."

Melissa interrupted with a loud laugh. "Your dad won't do anything. Believe me, I own most of his people now. And the rest..." She shrugged, suggesting that they no longer mattered.

Jordan had to hope one of her gang members was still loyal to Mr. Goss. He had to hope that person would slink away and phone Mr. Goss secretly. Jordan needed

Amy's father to come and rescue them because he couldn't see any other means of escape. Both of Melissa Pink's bodyguards had trained their guns on him. He might be able to deflect one bullet, but he'd be helpless against two fired at the same time.

But Melissa Pink was even more cold-hearted than he thought.

She turned to her minders and said, "No, no, no! Don't aim at him. Aim at her." She jabbed a finger towards Amy.

Clearing her nose with a grotesque sniff, she grinned at Jordan. "Maybe you can protect yourself, but you can't protect her. Try anything and she gets it. Understand?"

Jordan nodded.

"Someone should've told you the problem with friends and family," Melissa said as she waved some men into the gap between the silos. "Caring about someone makes you vulnerable."

Coming up behind him, two men grabbed Jordan by the shoulders.

Melissa pointed at one of the strong metal struts. "Use the towrope to tie his right arm to one of them. Then attach it to the tractor." She gazed into Jordan's face. "When we put it in reverse, you'll be disarmed. Literally." She laughed at her own malicious joke.

Realizing the true horror of his situation, Jordan flinched as the men dragged him to the side, attached his artificial arm to the metal rod, and then looped the rope around a bar across the front of the tractor. If the bolts in his arm were weaker than the bones of his shoulder, the arm would wrench off without damaging him. If the bolts held firm, the tractor could wrench the bone out of his body.

Amy had worked it out as well. There was terror in her eyes.

Melissa did not react. She was simply doing what she did best. "We've got unfinished business, you and me. It's time it was dealt with. But I've learned to be careful. You're dangerous with that arm. Let's see what you're like without it. You know, in the good old days, bad guys had their arms and legs tied to horses that were made to gallop off in different directions. Being pulled apart was a spectator sport back then. So's this, I guess."

He shut his eyes and braced himself as the engine started to clatter.

The tractor clunked into gear, revved, and then jerked backwards. The rope lifted off the ground.

Jordan recalled Angel's words in his mind. "You don't give up." It was true. So, why had he closed his eyes and accepted what was about to happen?

He looked down at his fake arm as the rope became taut. At once, he saw what he had to do. He couldn't stop what was about to happen but he could lessen the damage – and the pain. He crooked his arm so that its elbow joint nestled against the strut. That way, the elbow and metal support would take the full force, instead of his shoulder.

The rope tightened and tugged but he kept still, making sure his arm wasn't dragged out of position. He concentrated on bending his elbow firmly around the metal rod. The tension increased and he felt the strain on his shoulder, but that's all it was. A dull ache, not pain. The elbow joint creaked as if it were being crushed in a vice.

His gut told him to expect agony and blood but his brain told him that flesh and bone weren't coming apart. It was only metal, carbon fibre and wire.

There was a massive crunch and a jolt. By instinct, Jordan cried out as his forearm detached at the elbow.

His hand and lower arm flew in one direction and he collapsed in the other.

Above him, Melissa Pink scratched her nose and said, "Not as spectacular as I'd hoped. But it's good enough. You can't do much damage with a stump." She shouted to her men, "Tie them both up, gag them, and sling them in the back of the van. Leave the arm here in case anyone comes looking for him. A nice little warning about what happens to people who cross me."

20 TORTURED

The ride in the van was horrible. He lay on the hard metal floor, barely able to breathe because of the tape across his mouth. Each time the van went round a corner, he rocked sideways. When it braked or accelerated sharply, he slid up and down. His sweatshirt hung limply from the smashed elbow, reminding him how helpless he felt without his forearm.

But that discomfort was nothing compared with Amy's angry face. She made him feel awful. Also gagged, she was trying to communicate with her eyes. They were very expressive. "How can you still be alive?" she was saying. "What was your funeral all about? Why do you look so different? WHY DIDN'T YOU TELL ME?"

Jordan felt tortured by his dishonesty towards her, yet how could he have explained what had happened to him? The truth was too complicated, too hush-hush and probably too dangerous. He'd made a deal with Angel never to contact her, never to reveal who he really was. He didn't want her to vanish off the face of the planet like Deborah Metland.

At least he could be open and honest with her from now on because she knew who he was. But then would she want to stay friends? And did they have any hope of a future?

Jordan wanted to get himself and Amy out of this mess on his own. He didn't want to rely on Unit Red, especially when he was determined to keep Amy secret. But they were in big trouble. He had little choice. Concentrating enough to log on to the Unit Red computer was difficult under the circumstances. It took him three attempts to gain access. Then he left a message. *In a van, kidnapped by Melissa Pink. Arm broken. No idea where going. Will update when I can.*

What would Angel make of that? He'd know what was

happening, but what could he do about it? To attempt any sort of rescue, he'd have to know where Jordan was. But Jordan didn't have a clue. There were no windows in the back of the van.

Winter stood between the silos with half of Jordan's arm in her hand. The GPS device that revealed Jordan's location at all times was in this part of his false arm. Into her phone, she said, "No, it's not Jordan. It's the section from the hand to the elbow. That's all."

"Is there any blood on it?" asked Angel.

"No. They've detached it at the elbow. He's probably okay. But we've lost our trace. Has he got his mobile on?"

"No."

"So, unless he can tell us where he is, he's on his own."

"That's not the only problem," Angel replied.

"I know," Winter said.

After Jordan's robotic hand had been damaged by caustic, Angel had ordered a GPS chip to be inserted under the new silicone skin when his right arm had been de-gloved. Then, after the Hunstanton incident, Angel had decided that tracking Jordan's position wasn't enough. He'd told the technician who had tested Jordan's false arm to slip a microphone secretly into the thumb. Unit Red had heard everything that had been said among the grain silos.

"We need to find Jordan," Angel said. "And we need to find Amy Goss. Then you're going to have to deal with her, Winter. We can't afford another security risk."

The tyre noise changed. The van was driving over gravel when it came to a sudden halt. The rear doors banged open, daylight stung Jordan's eyes, and he was bundled outside. He was standing on a stony path that led to a simple and isolated jetty. He didn't recognize the area. There were bushes on either side but no buildings within sight and the shoreline showed no distinguishing features. Melissa's men were pouring out of a second van. Within seconds, Jordan was marched towards a rundown fishing boat, an armed guard on each side of him. Melissa was in front, Amy was behind.

They were shoved on board and pushed roughly onto smelly upturned crates that had once held the boat's catch. The wheelhouse was at the front and the stern was full of rusting equipment for catching, handling and storing fish. A metal arch with pulleys and dangling ropes bridged the two sides of the boat. In one corner, there were some rotting fish-heads.

Melissa smiled spitefully at Jordan and said, "Look around. We've got hooks, winches, chains, rope, nets, all sorts of instruments. Any of them could be used imaginatively to make you talk. And, believe me, I can be very inventive."

Jordan shuddered. He could see how a traditional trawler could easily become a torture chamber. While he glanced around he also engaged his terahertz vision. Three of Melissa's men had concealed knives and the other two were carrying guns. As he lowered his eyes, he noticed that the bald and bearded minder had a second gun in a holster strapped to the bottom of his leg, just above his right ankle. There was also a knife attached to his left leg. Having encountered Jordan in the sports club, he was taking no chances this time.

Jordan recognized three of the men who had tried to dunk him in caustic solution. One had an ugly scar on his cheek and Jordan wondered if he'd caused the wound when he'd flung the corrosive liquid at them. The thug deserved it, but was no doubt hungry to get even now.

Melissa shouted to someone in the wheelhouse, "Okay. Let's head out."

One of the crew untied the mooring ropes and the engine throbbed louder. The fishing boat made for deep water.

Jordan forced his mind to go online. It wasn't easy to stay alert and, at the same time, think his password into the Unit Red system. Once again, it took several attempts. As soon as he logged on, he left another message. *On an old fishing boat at sea. No idea where.* It wasn't a helpful message, but he had to do something. As an afterthought, he added, *They've got guns.* He did not sign out of the system.

He glanced at Amy. Her expression was a mixture of fear and defiance. He wondered where her loyalties now lay. If Melissa Pink quizzed her about him, what would she say? Would Amy lie for him or would she blurt out all that she knew? Jordan wasn't sure. He was familiar only with the younger Amy. That Amy would never have betrayed Ben Smith. But Jordan Stryker had duped this Amy and she knew it. She owed him nothing. She might even bear him a grudge.

Melissa stood up straight and sniffed the sea air. "Ah. Bracing." She turned to her captives and said, "I like boats. You're out in the open, but no one sees or hears. And no one escapes. If anyone happens to realize where you are, we can see them coming from a long way off."

She nodded at her bald bodyguard and he seemed to understand what she wanted. He stepped forward, untied them and yanked the sticky tape from both of their mouths.

Jordan let out a quiet yelp and swallowed a couple of times. Amy spat over the side of the trawler.

"Now mobiles," Melissa added.

The same thug went through their pockets and extracted their phones. Once he'd handed them to Melissa, she pitched them over her shoulder and into the sea. Then she sat down, well away from Jordan and Amy, rested her head on the rail and closed her eyes as if she were a tourist relaxing on a cruise.

It struck Jordan that Melissa avoided getting close to them as if she were scared of catching germs. When there had to be contact, she got her bouncers to step in. Perhaps it was her way of remaining superior. Perhaps she just didn't want to leave any evidence on her victims.

A few noisy and hopeful seagulls followed the trawler for a while, but they scattered as soon as they realized there were no fish to scavenge.

"How far can you swim? With a disability like yours," Melissa said, opening her eyes and staring at Jordan, "not far at all. But I don't know about you, young Goss.

So, I'm taking no chances. Let's have a chat when we've gone a bit further. The water's so cold out there even strong swimmers don't last long."

Jordan looked at what was left of his artificial arm. He sent a message to flex his fingers and, of course, nothing happened. Checking what movement he had still got, he found he could move the stump forwards and backwards – like the arm action of a marching soldier – but nothing more.

Amy watched him testing his right arm, but she said nothing.

Jordan knew she had plenty to say to him, but she'd stay silent while Melissa and her heavies hovered over them like big birds of prey.

After about twenty minutes, Melissa stood up again and went towards the wheelhouse. "That'll do," she said to someone inside. Then she returned to the rear of the boat.

Jordan's heart began to pound even more than before.

The trawler rocked gently and the engine chugged idly. Standing in the centre of the stern and facing Amy, Melissa jerked her thumb in Jordan's direction. "What do you know about him?"

"Almost nothing," Amy replied. "We bumped into each

other after your lot chased him out of the sports club a couple of weeks back." She shrugged. "That's it really."

"And from that sprang a beautiful relationship?"

"I wouldn't put it like that."

"How would you put it?"

Amy shrugged again. "He's all right. We met twice more."

"Did you ask to see him or was it the other way round?"

"He came to me."

Overhead, a commercial aircraft made its way noisily towards the mainland.

Melissa looked around again. No doubt she wanted to give the impression that she wasn't in a hurry. "Mmm. It's nice out here. Quite calm and sunny today. Can't see much of the land. I gave some of your dad's people a tour like this. It was their last chance to switch sides. The ones that didn't take it were counted as victims of the Thames explosion. Very convenient." She paused before adding, "That was somewhere different, you understand. We're nowhere near the estuary here."

Jordan wondered if that was the truth or a double bluff. He was desperate to find out where they were.

Abruptly, Melissa turned back to Amy. "You're hiding something."

Amy shook her head and then changed her mind. "Oh. He fancies himself as a hero. He dragged someone from a burning car. I was impressed with that. And he doesn't go to school. He gets home tuition."

"There's more."

"Er... He lost his real arm in a car accident."

Jordan recognized edginess in her voice. He guessed that she was nervous. He also thought that, inside, she was seething with rage.

"Put your mind to it," Melissa said as she fingered a large boathook. "You might come up with something worthwhile."

"I can't... No. There's one more thing." She glanced sideways at Jordan and said, "He lives next door to one of my teachers."

Melissa nodded. "You're not trying hard enough. Perhaps a bit of persuasion... But first..." She turned towards Jordan. "You puzzle me, Stryker. And I don't like puzzles. I like to know things. If a member of the great British public has their arm ripped off in a car crash, the NHS doesn't provide a false one like yours. They get something tinny and basic. It makes them feel better about themselves and makes it easier for the rest of us to look at them and forget they got hurt. They don't get what you've got – or what you had. That's a lot more than basic. It's very special. A lethal weapon. So, someone's backing you with money and power. Maybe it's not young Amy's dad. Maybe I was wrong." She paused. "I don't like being wrong any more than I like puzzles. So, talk to me. Explain."

The guard with the shaggy beard stood to her left and the second stood to her right, next to a crate of dirty nets. Both men were still holding guns. One was trained on Amy, the other on Jordan.

He decided to throw Melissa a titbit. He hoped it might satisfy her curiosity. "All right. My arm came off in the Thames explosion..."

"I'm not stupid. I'd guessed that."

"I wanted to find out who mashed me up so I started asking..."

Melissa interrupted again. "It's the bit in between that interests me. You can't do that without backup. If it's not Goss's outfit, who's behind you? I want to know. I want to know who patched you up and told you to start asking questions about the bombing."

Jordan shook his head.

She sighed loudly. Bending down, she picked up an old, rusting fish hook from one of the equipment chests and then fiddled with it in her hand. "Have you ever wondered about fish?" she asked. "I have. It's the way we catch them. Not nets. When we hook them with this sort of thing." She held out the vicious barbed hook. "It goes right through the cheek. Is it called a cheek if you're a fish? Anyway, I bet it hurts when we pull them out of the sea."

Jordan didn't respond. He didn't know what to say. All he knew was that he was afraid.

"This is a good opportunity for some research. If we try it on you, we'll soon find out." She handed the hook to one of her henchmen.

It was the bald guy. He put his gun back inside his jacket and, holding the hook in his right hand, advanced eagerly on Jordan. He was about to grab Jordan's jaw with his nicotine-stained left fingers, when he hesitated. "His eyes are funny, boss. Know what I mean?"

"Are they?" she replied, but she didn't take a close look herself. "What's going on with them?" she asked Jordan. "Have you had something done to them?"

Jordan swallowed before he could talk. "They got scratched and stuff. I had to have an operation to put them right."

"What else have you had done?" she demanded to know.

"Nothing else like my arm, if that's what you mean. Just lots of operations."

Melissa smiled. "You're like some ageing celebrity. Cosmetic surgeons crawling all over you. Someone wanted you in good condition for a reason. Undress him. Let's take a look."

Jordan shrank back.

"Come on," she said. "Don't be shy. If you resist, it'll be worse. We'll tie you up in nets."

They yanked off his top and trousers, but at least they left him in his pants. They dragged him to his feet and prowled around, examining him as if he were some sort of exhibit or freak.

The thug with the disfigured face said, "There's something in his leg." He reached for the knife that was concealed inside his leather jacket.

"No!" Jordan recoiled even before the guy got it out.

Melissa exclaimed, "You know he's got a knife! How?"

"I don't," Jordan lied. "It's just that... It's not hard to guess. He looked like he was going to cut me up."

Melissa wasn't entirely satisfied, but she didn't pursue it. "What's in your leg?"

"It's a battery. That's all. It powers my arm."

"Do you see yourself as some sort of James Bond? He had lots of gadgets." She laughed. "That makes me a Bond villain. But they were all fools. They strapped our

James into some contraption to kill him and then left, giving him time and opportunity to escape. That's not me. I'm not going anywhere. I'm staying right here till the job's done." Checking with her heavies, she asked, "Nothing else bionic and dangerous?"

"No. Just lots of scars."

Luckily his brain implants weren't obvious. His hair hid the marks.

"Carry on with the experiment."

The bald thug looked puzzled.

"To find out if it hurts when you're hooked. I've got a hunch it's as painful as it looks, but we'd better make sure."

The bouncer's face creased into a repulsive smile. He forced Jordan's jaws apart with the foul stained fingers of his left hand. Enjoying himself, he shoved the barbed hook into Jordan's mouth with his right.

Flinching, Amy looked away.

21 UNDERWATER

"All right!" Jordan choked over his words because of the dirty fingers in his mouth. "I'll tell you the truth."

Melissa nodded at the gangster and, denied the chance to torture Jordan, he stepped back, disappointed.

Jordan steadied himself and, head down, took a few deep breaths. The horrible taste lingered in his mouth. Another aeroplane emerged out of the cloud when he looked up. "My mum was in the police. When my family died in the estuary explosion, the police looked after me.

They asked me to find out what happened as a sort of payback for patching me up."

Melissa didn't reply at first. She simply stared at him. Then she shook her head. "You're holding back. Those crazy eyes tell me there's more. And I don't believe in the Police Youth Squad for a second."

The captain called from the wheelhouse. "Low-flying helicopter coming in!"

Melissa did not have to give any orders. The crew executed a routine that was as practised as a school fire drill. Within seconds, Jordan and Amy had been tossed roughly into separate crates and covered with nets. Men stood over them with knives, pretending to mend the nets. One crew member operated the winch and two more pretended to ready the fishing tackle. Melissa was out of sight in the wheelhouse. From above, the trawler would seem to be going about its business of catching fish.

From the coffin-like box, Jordan could not see very much. He heard the helicopter approach, he saw it flash past, and he listened to the fading sound of its rotors with a sinking feeling.

But, while he lay there in his underwear, before the torture began again, he thought another message onto Angel's computer. *Was that Winter in a helicopter? It just came close.*

Angel must have been online because, in his mind, Jordan saw an immediate response. *No.*

Can't you use it to find out where I am?

What type was it?

Not sure. Something like Coastal Rescue written down the side.

Angel's typed reply appeared gradually in his mind. *Good. I'll get onto the Coastguard and find out where they've got a chopper in the air.*

We're on a flight path as well. Two planes have gone overhead about ten minutes apart.

Leaving or coming in to land?

Heading inland.

That'll help to fix your position. I'm working on it.

As two men dragged him out of the crate, Jordan lost contact with Unit Red but, for the first time, he sensed hope. He tried not to show it, though.

"I'm sick of the sight of you like that," Melissa said to Jordan. "Get dressed."

It wasn't easy to put his clothes back on with one hand and a stump.

When he'd finished, she stood in front of him and Amy, glancing from one to the other with a sneer on her pale face. "Sorry about the interruption. I think we can resume our session now." She scratched at her nose and sniffed loudly. "What if I said only one of you is going to survive? Who'd volunteer to go under to save the other? It's interesting to speculate, isn't it? And it'd be fun to find out." Fixing her eyes on Amy, she continued, "If he's only chatted you up three times and there's nothing between you, it won't upset you much to see him die. That's no use." She shifted her gaze to Jordan, "So, I'll let you watch her die. That'll get things moving because you're the type to get upset. Perfect."

Melissa gave another of her knowing nods. This time, it was directed at the man standing by the winch.

"It's a variation on waterskiing, I suppose," she announced. "Only it happens under the water. And, believe me, your dad's men couldn't take it. Not a single one. Let's see how you get on."

Two men held out Amy's arms and tied the dangling steel cables around her wrists. The winch squealed into action, the cables ran through the pulleys on the arched frame and lifted her off the deck by her outstretched arms. Her body formed a Y shape.

It must have felt as if she was being torn apart, but Amy didn't give any of them the satisfaction of screaming or crying.

Talking to Jordan, Melissa said, "This is going to be painful for you to watch. But that's nothing compared to the pain she's feeling. And when she goes overboard? Excruciating."

Jordan glared at the gangland boss and decided that she was a monster.

Reading the hatred in his expression, Melissa Pink shrugged. "It's strange but true. I've always enjoyed violence."

"As long as you don't have to do it yourself," Jordan muttered.

"No one keeps dogs and barks themselves."

"What?"

"There's no point paying all these people around me and doing the dirty work myself." She nodded towards Amy, suspended a metre above the deck. "You can save her, you know. You can open up and convince me you've told me everything."

Jordan didn't believe her. He thought she enjoyed killing too much to let either of them go. Perhaps caving in and confessing everything about Unit Red would buy them an easier and quicker death, but he was convinced that she would not let them walk away from this boat trip.

He was no longer online. His brain could not cope with what was about to happen to Amy and maintain a link to Angel at the same time. He didn't know what he could do. If he tried to make any sort of move, he'd be gunned down before he took two steps. The bald guy would see to that. He was itching to pull the trigger, not once but lots of times. The gangster would love to see Jordan go down in a storm of bullets. And he was so close, he couldn't miss.

Melissa called out to Amy, "We're going to throw you out like a net. Then we're going to power the boat up and take you for a ride. Hold your breath but, to be honest, you won't last long whatever you do. The water's forced into your mouth, nose and lungs. Then it's goodbye. It's also agony, I'm told. Very unpleasant. You might last the first twenty or thirty seconds. No more." Melissa sighed as if she regretted what she was about to do. "Have you got anything to say before you go over?"

Amy strained her neck so that she could look at Jordan for a few seconds before she answered. "No. I don't do deals with you. Not for anyone."

Amy was not going to reveal who he really was. Jordan didn't know if she was keeping quiet because of the friendship they'd once shared or because she despised Melissa Pink.

He saw something other than bravery and contempt in her face. Silently, she was imploring him to be the hero once more. After all, he was the one who'd pulled a driver from a burning car. Surely he could grab Amy and save her from this ordeal. Yet, without his right arm, Jordan didn't feel like a hero. He felt disabled, helpless and outwitted.

He didn't know how to pay back her silence.

Melissa waved a hand dismissively. "Give her a taster. Five seconds should do it."

The boat's engine coughed and snarled. The trawler began to carve its way through the waves. The men put their guns inside their jackets and pushed Amy out over the stern with poles. At once, the cables lowered her down out of Jordan's view. He heard the splash, though. He also heard himself shout, "No!"

22 WEAPONS

In a state of extreme distress, Amy was choking and spluttering when she reappeared seconds later. Writhing on the end of the line, water ran from her shoes, her school uniform, her hair and her mouth.

Jordan had never seen such suffering. It was unbearable to watch. Yet he was the only one on the trawler who was sickened. Some of them were relishing her torment. Jordan could not understand how they could be so pitiless. They were less than human.

He could not help himself. Revolted by such brutality, he staggered towards her.

Almost immediately, both of Pink's bodyguards had him by the shoulders. They held him so that he had no option but to look at Amy as she dripped and swayed in the air, suspended cruelly by steel ropes.

Behind him, Melissa said, "Would I be right in assuming you're ready to talk?"

"Yes," he said in a broken voice. "Let her go. It's got nothing to do with Amy. She doesn't know anything."

Melissa laughed. "I don't think you're in much of a position to bargain. Just tell me who you're working for."

The minders shuffled him round until he faced their boss.

"Come on. Come on. Or she goes over again."

The engine had slowed again and the trawler was drifting on the tide.

Jordan's legs quivered, hardly able to support his weight. "I feel ill..."

Melissa groaned impatiently. "When you invaded my club, you opted to join the big bad adult world, Stryker. You can't act like a little kid now. It was your choice."

But Jordan's head flopped forward and his body went limp.

Melissa cursed. "Drop him," she ordered. "And someone fetch me a bucket of cold water to chuck over him."

The men let go and Jordan crashed to the deck.

The remainder of his false arm hit first. His hips and head thudded onto the surface that had once teemed with fish.

The heavies relaxed, shook their heads at each other, and then laughed.

It was the off-guard moment that Jordan had anticipated. He reached out with his left hand for the bearded thug's right ankle. In one swift movement, he pulled the man's gun out of its holster and jumped up. In a second, he was at Melissa's side, holding the revolver to her head.

Taken by surprise, both bodyguards drew their weapons and aimed at him, but they didn't fire. They looked to Melissa for instructions.

Jordan whispered in her ear, "Don't try anything. I'm already shaking. It wouldn't take much to make this thing go off." He moved behind her and swung the upper part of his fake arm around her throat. "Put your guns down," he said to her bouncers. "No. Throw them overboard. I can shoot her or strangle her. It's only half an arm but it'll crush her neck in a split second."

"Idiots," Melissa croaked. "How could you let a school kid...?"

"Throw them into the sea!" Jordan yelled.

Melissa could barely nod but, when she did, her minders obeyed him.

The sound of the two sploshes came as a huge relief. Jordan hardly dared to believe that he was in control. But the ability and opportunity to kill in an instant gave him power. It was a power that terrified him. To beat Melissa Pink and her mob, though, he had to exploit his newfound authority.

He'd never handled a real gun before. DS Smith – his mother – had kept him well away from firearms. She hadn't even let him play with toy guns when he was a kid. Now, he didn't know what he was doing, but it didn't matter as long as Melissa Pink and her heavies believed he could pull the trigger. It didn't matter as long as they believed he *would* pull the trigger.

Shouting to the men at the stern, he said, "Let Amy down. Untie her. Or else." He tightened his grip on Melissa's throat and she let out a gurgle. His left hand was trembling so much that the barrel of the small revolver vibrated against her head. He could feel her cringing in his grip. He sensed that she was infuriated by his threats and disgusted by his nearness.

Melissa nodded slightly again and the men lowered the boat's wretched catch onto the deck and released her.

Amy didn't get up. She lay on the floor, washed up and exhausted. She seemed to be out cold.

"Now what?" Melissa rasped.

Jordan didn't know. He hadn't thought beyond getting Amy safely back into the trawler.

"You can't win," Melissa struggled to say. "One disabled boy and an unconscious girl against us all. One little slip and..."

"Shut up," Jordan said. He needed to think.

He could freeze. Play for time. Until Unit Red traced his position. But what if Angel couldn't pinpoint him? What if help didn't arrive? He couldn't hold a gun to Melissa Pink's head for ever. In front of him, there was a bunch of men – several holding knives – itching to impress their boss by taking him down. The only part of his body that was not quaking with fear was the stump of his arm.

Still flat out on the deck, Amy stirred, but no one noticed because she wasn't the centre of attention any more.

Jordan looked around and his eyes lingered on the lifeboat suspended from a small crane on the port side.

He wondered if he could use it to escape with Amy. But making a getaway in it wasn't that simple. He could exchange Melissa Pink for the lifeboat, but she'd order the trawler to ram them afterwards. They wouldn't stand a chance. To save themselves from this standoff, they'd have to take the gang's leader with them in the lifeboat. She would be their insurance against attack.

"We're going in the lifeboat," he announced. "Someone help Amy in."

Melissa's eyes told them to do as he said.

When two of the men lifted Amy by her shoulders, she looked up. At once, panic came to her face. "Behind!" she spluttered.

For a moment, Jordan didn't realize what she meant. Then he spun round awkwardly, still clutching Melissa Pink.

The captain had emerged from the wheelhouse and was creeping up silently behind Jordan. He was swinging the boathook at Jordan's head.

Jordan ducked and put up his metal stump to protect himself, but he wasn't quick enough. The heavy hook thwacked against his arm and then smacked into his forehead. Jordan's world turned upside down.

Melissa sprang away from him and the gun flew from his left hand. It skittered across the deck.

The men holding Amy dropped her and reached for the weapon. But, sprawled on the deck, Amy was closer. She grabbed it, rolled over, and then jumped to her feet. Staggering, she couldn't keep her balance at first. Trying to make her eyes focus, she steadied herself and aimed at Melissa Pink.

But Melissa was smiling again. She was smiling because the bald minder was behind Jordan, holding a knife to his neck. "You're almost as dazed as he is," she said. "Put it down, young Goss, or your boyfriend..."

"He's not my boyfriend," Amy replied.

"You're bluffing."

"I don't know him and I don't care what..."

Melissa interrupted. "Let's see." To her bodyguard, she said, "I've had enough. Kill him."

The brute's black hole of a mouth curved into a smirk.

Jordan was vaguely aware of the thug's beard tickling his neck. Then the prickle became a scratch and the scratch became a sting. The blade cut into his skin.

Amy changed her line of sight. She blinked once to clear her vision and then fired.

Jordan could almost see the bullet coming. He was a huge target and over his shoulder was the gangster's bald head. A tiny bull's-eye in comparison. Jordan heard the bullet zip past his ear. It punctured the man's brow and crashed its way destructively out of the back of his skull.

He was dead before the knife fell from his hand.

For an instant, Melissa looked surprised. Then she said, "So, your dad made sure his family could shoot straight. A wise precaution." She didn't seem concerned in the slightest about her bodyguard, whose blood was pooling massively on the deck.

Still clearly light-headed, Amy also seemed surprised by her success. She pointed the weapon at Melissa again.

Melissa glanced at the two men closest to Amy. "Disarm her," she ordered.

Her henchmen looked at each other but did not risk going up to Amy.

"Disarm her, I said!"

"They don't seem keen," Amy muttered. "I'll tell you the difference between me and B...Jordan. He just threatened you. No real reason to do more than that. But me? I've got a really good excuse to kill you. This is for my dad and all those men you..."

Melissa turned, zigzagged across the deck and leaped over the safety rail.

By the time Amy fired, she was out of sight.

They all made for that side of the trawler and leaned against the rail.

"Where is she?" one of her gangsters cried.

"I can't see nothing."

"She's not coming up."

They waited anxiously, scanning the surface.

There was nothing but the gentle stroke of waves against the boat's flank.

"She's gone under!"

"No one lasts long in there. She said so herself. It's too cold."

"Her clothes must have dragged her down."

The skipper steered the trawler hard to starboard and turned a complete circle. They saw nothing.

Dumbfounded, Melissa's men stared at one other. None of them was willing to go overboard in a crazy attempt to save their leader.

Amy was still clutching the gun with both hands, but she had drooped. She was no longer capable of lifting it and firing again.

Two of the gangsters advanced menacingly towards her.

Standing protectively beside her, the scarred thug shouted, "No! Think about it. There'll be a reward for taking her back."

"Reward? What are you talking about?"

"Her father's the biggest thing in town again now. If we take her back, he'll reward us with a job. Goss'll pay our wages."

"Yeah. Good point."

There was a murmur of agreement.

"So, what do we do now?"

He shouted to the captain, "It's all over here. Pink's had it. Gone. Take us back."

"Okay. But first, get that lump overboard," he said, pointing at the body of the minder. "And wash down the deck. I don't want a trace left by the time we get ashore."

There was no sentiment in Melissa Pink's world. A couple of the men rolled the body over the side and then swilled away the stain as if they were cleaning up after hooking an unwanted fish.

Jordan was concussed. He could barely stand. In his mind, the boat wasn't pitching calmly. It seemed to be turning right over. He leaned over the side and vomited.

He didn't notice the blood trickling from the top of his head and his neck. He wiped his mouth and somehow felt a little better for being sick. He gazed at Amy. She seemed to sway from side to side. He knew he'd lost control of the full range of his vision because she had an infrared glow. At times, her wet clothes muted some of the yellowy-red colour, then they dissolved from his sight altogether. To Jordan, she was an unstable ghost.

"I'm sorry, Amy," he said weakly. "I can explain."

Amy shook her head. "Not now, you can't. You look like you're about to pass out." She paused before mumbling, "You're not the only one feeling wrecked. I've just killed a man."

While the trawler made for the jetty, where their journey had begun, Jordan sat near Amy on an upside-down crate. Melissa's heavies kept an eye on them but said nothing and didn't bother them. Amy kept the small gun on her lap.

Jordan knew he had to do something. Yes. He had to contact Unit Red. He had to update Angel. But he wasn't sure if his brain/computer interface was still functioning. Nothing seemed to respond normally. When he thought he was online, he tried to leave the message: *Heading back to land. Melissa Pink drowned.* But he could have uploaded a meaningless jumble of words – or nothing at all – into his section of the system. He wasn't sure.

If he had been thinking clearly, he would have asked the captain where they were so that he could inform Unit

Red. But his head wound made him woozy. He was still hoping that Angel had figured out their position from his aircraft sightings and that help was already on its way.

He turned towards Amy and whispered, "Will your dad give this lot jobs?"

"Not a chance. He'll go ballistic – to put it mildly – when I tell him they tortured me. On top of that, they switch sides way too easily. But I'm not letting on till they get me back."

Jordan nodded. He took a deep breath, swallowed, and tried again. "Amy. There's a reason I couldn't tell you…"

She shook her head. "There's never a reason to lie to your best friend."

Jordan gave up.

In the distance, the landing stage came into view.

There was no threat when the men ushered Jordan and Amy off the trawler and onto the jetty. One of them even asked Amy if she was feeling better. The mood was very different from when they'd been shoved onto the boat.

The gangsters shambled along the pontoon towards the two vans, but Jordan and Amy hung back as if they didn't want to admit they belonged to the same bunch.

Nearing the first van, the men suddenly froze. Four armed people had stepped out from behind it.

Further back, Jordan's heart stopped for a moment. A second later, he let out a sigh. Despite his distorted vision, he recognized Winter and three agents.

"It's okay," he told Amy. "They're on our side."

Within seconds, the Unit Red team had stripped the gang members of their knives, forced them into the second van, and locked them inside. Winter instructed the agents to take them all to the nearest police station. "I'll look after Jordan and Amy," she announced, putting her gun away.

She walked towards Jordan at the edge of the jetty and said, "Sorry it took so long to find you, but it looks like you didn't need us. Again. Good work." She peered at his head and neck wounds with concern before glancing at Amy and noting the gun in her fist. "Are you both all right?"

They were exhausted, bruised and bedraggled, but they nodded anyway.

"I think you'd better give me that," she said to Amy, holding out her hand for the gun.

"No," Amy snapped, clinging on to it protectively. "I don't know you."

Winter was about to insist, but seemed to think Amy

was in a fragile and possibly unstable state. "Okay. You keep it safe." Instead, she turned round. "Come on. Let's get you both sorted out." She strode up the gravel path.

Melissa's hands were numb and white with cold. She could no longer cling to the trawler's rope. She lowered herself into the water and swam to the shore. Hearing voices near the jetty, she ducked down behind a bush and waited for an opportunity.

23 REVENGE

Refusing to move, Amy nodded towards Winter and asked, "Who's she?"

Jordan smiled nervously. "Her name's Winter."

"What sort of a name is that?"

"She's okay," Jordan said. "Really."

"I bet it's a name like Jordan Stryker. Made up. Does she know who you are?"

Jordan nodded. Keeping his voice down, he said, "But it's important you don't let her know that you do as well. *Very* important."

Amy didn't ask why. She was still too annoyed. She also looked worried. "Is she some sort of cop? Is she going to ask what I did on the boat?"

"It's all right," Jordan replied as the trawler chugged away from the jetty. "No one's going to blame you. Trust me..."

"Trust you? How can I trust you now?"

"I'll explain, Amy. At least, I'll try. Honest. Jordan Stryker, Winter, everything. But not here. Not now." Noticing that his Unit Red handler had disappeared into the van, Jordan said to Amy, "Come on. Winter'll take us home."

But Amy stayed where she was, looking at the revolver in her hand. Making up her mind, she drew her arm back, ready to launch the evidence into the sea.

She was about to throw it as far as she could when someone behind her snatched the weapon from her grasp.

Jordan twisted round and gasped in shock as he came face-to-face with Melissa Pink. The gang leader had sneaked out from the bushes and for once touched one of her enemies. In a slick move, she hooked one arm around Amy's neck and pushed the barrel of the gun against her head with the other.

It was exactly how Jordan had threatened Melissa Pink on the trawler.

She dragged her victim a few steps away from Jordan. Her expression was contorted with rage and she was dripping seawater like blood. Her long hair was flattened against her head and shoulders. A tangled piece of seaweed gave her a bizarre green ribbon. She was shaking and wild growling noises came from her nose and throat. But she also looked triumphant.

Jordan was numb. He thought that Melissa was going to kill Amy right there in front of him, just three or four metres away. She was certainly in the mood to kill someone.

Slowly, her mouth curved into a smile and she shook her head at him. "No, I'm not going to shoot your precious girlfriend. Not yet."

With horror, Jordan watched Melissa turn the gun towards him until it was pointing straight at his face. That cold metal barrel was all he saw. It blanked out everything else from his vision. The last thing he would see was an emerging bullet and a puff of smoke.

Melissa Pink milked the moment. "This is so easy," she said. "No challenge at all, but immensely satisfying." She squeezed the trigger.

Two loud bangs made Jordan jump. But there was no

pain, no sudden impact. Just two gunshots echoing in his head like a death knell.

First, Amy slumped forwards and then Melissa jerked sideways. Both crumpled onto the wooden surface of the jetty.

Still groggy, Jordan couldn't work out exactly what had happened. He saw Winter sprinting from the van to the jetty. He heard her shout, "I had no choice." He saw blood spreading. Some of it was his, coming from his open wounds. The rest collected between Amy and Melissa.

Amy had rolled oddly onto her back. Her arms and legs were splayed out on the ground. She seemed to be staring up at the sky. But she wasn't. Her eyes had glazed over.

That was all that Jordan saw. Shock and exhaustion got the better of him. He blacked out.

On one side of Jordan was a stone angel, standing on a plinth. Like Jordan, the winged boy was missing a right arm. On the other side was a row of grubby headstones at odd angles. They reminded him of rotten teeth.

He imagined that, when she was thirteen, Amy would have gone to his funeral. Yet he was still here. Alive.

Lying on the ground of Highgate Cemetery. And where was Amy? Lying on a cold slab in a pathology laboratory. But Jordan would not be able to go to her funeral when her body was released to her family. He could not risk the Goss family asking him difficult questions.

Jordan thumped the earth. He had died and come back to life. He could not get used to the idea that Amy would not do the same. The bullet had done too much damage. Modern medicine had come to his rescue, but apparently it couldn't help Amy.

In his head, Jordan could still hear Winter's explanation of what she had done. "I was by the van. Melissa Pink was about to kill you. I couldn't let that happen, Jordan. But she was holding Amy in front of her. I had to go through Amy. It was a snap decision. There was no other way."

Winter had been totally successful. Her first bullet had passed through Amy's body and wounded Melissa before she could fire. A moment later, the second had killed the gangster outright.

Amy was no longer a security risk. No longer an embarrassment to Unit Red. She was no longer upset with Jordan. No longer waiting for an explanation for his strange behaviour and appearance. She was no longer his secret friend.

His shoulders shaking, Jordan took a deep breath and closed his eyes. He could not escape the thought that, if he'd really died and been buried in a place like this cemetery, Amy would still be alive. But he'd cheated death and somehow they'd swapped fates. He felt guilty, nauseous and numb. He felt that the world was carrying on without him.

Still grieving for his old friend, Jordan slumped into a chair in the bunker. He didn't even have half a right arm any more. The upper part had been unscrewed from his shoulder and removed for repair. Once fixed, it would be reattached to the forearm that Winter had rescued from the ground between the silos. Then he would get a complete refit.

It seemed that Angel was saying sorry to him for the hundredth time. "I can't tell you how much I regret what happened. It's always dreadful when an innocent life... I know Amy meant a lot..."

The estuary explosion had damaged Jordan's eyes but apparently it had not damaged his tear ducts. He felt tears welling up yet again. "Winter shot Amy. It wasn't an accident. But you said killing's never the first choice."

"That's perfectly true, Jordan. But we've been through this before. Melissa Pink wasn't drowned. She was alive with a firearm. She turned it on you and she was about to fire. Did you have any doubt she was going to kill you?"

"No," Jordan admitted.

"That's not a situation Winter could tolerate. Shooting was her *only* choice. It was justified and I would have done the same."

Of course, it wasn't the story that had emerged in the news. The gangster, Melissa Pink, had shot a rival's daughter and then a police marksman had shot her. No mention of Winter, Jordan or Unit Red.

"But did she have to..."

"I'm afraid so. If Pink had been taller than Amy, Winter would have had a line of sight for a head shot. But she wasn't. Holding Amy in front of her, there was no direct target." Sympathetically, Angel added, "Look, I can't make you feel any better about it, but I've got some good news."

Jordan did not show any interest.

Carrying on, Angel said, "Forensics analysed the metal fragments of Lightfoot's *Windsong* bomb. They were identical to the parts salvaged from the device planted on the wreck of the *Richard Montgomery*."

At once, Jordan looked up. "So, there's a link to the estuary blast?"

"A strong link. And you were right about a remote control. They got it out of the River Crouch. It's a type that would have been capable of setting off the Thames bomb. So, that's the physical evidence that wraps it up. You got your man. I'm impressed."

Jordan closed his eyes for a moment and, despite everything, allowed himself to feel relieved that he had uncovered the truth. Then he looked at Angel. "I still want to go and see him."

Angel shook his head. "The answer's still the same. I wouldn't blame you – and I wouldn't be surprised – if you wanted to murder him."

"He wouldn't suffer if he died. And I want him to suffer."

"But you might change your mind when you get up close. I can't risk what you'd do. I have to bear in mind that, in a way, you're fitted with a lethal weapon."

That was what Melissa Pink had called his robotic arm. But Jordan looked down at his sagging sleeve. "I'm not at the moment."

Angel hesitated. "I suppose not."

"I've got to hear him admit what he's done."

"Will it really help – or just bring everything back?"

"It'll help."

Angel sighed and then took two deep breaths. "Well, I understand he's conscious now. If you go before your arm gets refitted..."

"Thanks."

"I want you to cool off for the rest of the day. I'll tell his police guard you're on your way tomorrow morning. They'll be under orders to stay outside, watching your every move."

"All right." Jordan's shrug was awkward and lopsided. "It's not like I'm going to do anything bad."

Norman Lightfoot was a very special patient. He had his own private room in the hospital. Two police officers were stationed permanently outside. One faced the corridor. One watched him through the glass. Both were armed. In a way, the hospital room was a prison cell, but its occupant was not capable of escaping or going anywhere.

Jordan had worked out for himself why the battered prisoner was under guard for twenty-four hours a day. If anyone found out who he was and what he'd done, the police might have to protect him from people bent on revenge. Norman Lightfoot would not be short of enemies. His police guards, like Angel, might even mistake Jordan for someone who wanted to take the law into his own hands.

But the law wasn't on Jordan's mind.

He walked slowly up to the bed and looked down on the feeble creature lying in it. Lightfoot wasn't like a rugby player any more. He looked broken.

In a way, Jordan had got what he wished for. He always wanted the bomber to go through the same pain and suffering as he had. Right now, Norman Lightfoot looked as hurt as Ben Smith had been.

His face was a curious purple colour. There were tubes everywhere. Some dripped liquids in, some took liquids away. Monitors beeped and hummed. The sound of suspended life. A fragile life, supported by machine and medicine. There was a strange smell of disinfectant and decay.

As Jordan watched in silence, Norman's eyes opened. They were dull like the eyes of a zombie in a horror film.

"Do you recognize me?" Jordan asked.

Lightfoot's head moved just a little. It was a faint nod.

"I never got to tell you that you destroyed my family. All dead. And you nearly killed me."

The eyes closed and then opened again. There was hurt in them, but Jordan wasn't sure if Lightfoot was feeling physical pain or the pain of remorse.

"I know you did it. The estuary explosion. There's forensic evidence. I need to hear you admit it."

There was no resistance left in this helpless stranded creature. He made the same movement again and his lips parted. A wispy voice said, "It was me. Yes."

Jordan shivered. "I know why you did it. To get your revenge on the company, the ship, the new captain and the crew."

The craggy head shifted again, acknowledging Jordan's words.

"It was nothing to do with me or my family. It was nothing to do with most of the people you killed. Why take it out on so many?"

"I didn't mean to..."

"You were just going for *Ocean Courage*?"

Tears formed in those dead eyes. He mumbled, "I didn't realize how big... I'm sorry."

So, he'd miscalculated. He wasn't quite the monster he could have been, but Jordan was still appalled. "There were thirty people on that ship."

"I'm sorry," he repeated.

"Do you think saying sorry makes things okay?"

His head rocked slightly from side to side.

"I could smash all this gear and pull the tubes out

in a couple of seconds. I'm glad I'd have to use my real arm. It'd feel good to do it with flesh and blood. The police and doctors would rush in, but I don't know if they'd be quick enough to save you. Let's face it. A lot of people would beg me to do it while I've got the chance. Don't you think I've got every right?"

"Yes," he croaked. The word was barely audible but Jordan could hear without leaning close to his mouth.

Jordan shook his head. "No chance. I'm not giving you an easy way out. And I hope no one else does." He hesitated and then said, "But what about you? Why did you set off the bomb on *Windsong*?"

"I was...I didn't know what I was doing."

"You weren't trying to kill yourself?"

"No."

"Good," said Jordan. "You'll get better. You'll learn to walk again. You'll have bad days. You'll hurt like hell, but not as much as the people whose lives you ruined by murdering their family and friends. You'll know how much they hate you, though. You'll feel their disgust. And they'll never forgive you. Never. You'll go to prison for the rest of your life." Determined to control his temper, Jordan gazed steadily into Norman Lightfoot's face. "You know what? I almost feel sorry for you."

His mission over, Jordan turned and left the room.

24 HIGHGATE

Jordan's robotic arm had been refitted. He had become whole again, yet in many ways he was still incomplete. His right hand could once more pick up a spider without killing it or smash violently through a door panel but, from shoulder to fingertip, it wasn't really his arm. He was living in the Highgate house, but it didn't really feel like home. He was safely among Angel and the other agents, but they were no substitute for Amy and his family.

Angel said to him, "You've done well. Better than I had any right to expect. I want you to be happy in Unit Red. So, now your arm's back in action, I've got something and someone to show you."

"Oh?"

"Here's your new ID."

At first glance, the small rectangle of plastic looked the same as the one he already had. Puzzled, Jordan asked, "What's different about it?"

"You've had a change of birthday. Same day, different year. You're seventeen."

Then it dawned on him. It was something that Winter had said to him when they'd first set out for Lower Stoke in her Audi. It seemed a long time ago.

Angel led the way down the stairs to the back of the house that faced Swain's Lane. At ground-level, there was a secure door. Once Angel had entered the code, he stood to one side and said, "After you."

Jordan reached out with his reconditioned right arm. Controlling the power so he didn't break the handle, he pulled the door open. What he saw inside wasn't simply a garage. It was a large area that could house three cars. Part of it was an engineering workshop. Ramps, computers, tyres, car parts, welding equipment, all sorts of contraptions. And two engineers. One of them had her back towards him but her head and shoulders were vaguely familiar. When Jordan and Angel entered and the door closed behind them, she turned round.

Open-mouthed, Jordan gasped.

"Hello, Jordan," she said. "Good to see you again."

Jordan was staring in disbelief at the missing firefighter and the woman who had saved his life. Unit Red had not killed her or exiled her in a foreign country. "You're Deborah..."

"She's our newest recruit," Angel said, interrupting. "And you're wrong about her name. She's Kate Stelfox. In a Unit Red sort of way."

Kate smiled at Jordan. "You and me, we've got something in common."

"Oh?"

"We've both got to leave a life behind."

"Why you?"

"Because I know too much about you. I had a choice. I could disappear to another country or I could join the club." She shrugged. "Here I am."

With a wry expression, Jordan nodded.

"Not much point dwelling on the past," she said. "Might as well enjoy what's in front of us."

Jordan knew it was true. He'd already got used to leaving Ben Smith behind, but it was hard to let Amy and his family go. Right now, one of his mum's mottos came to his mind. *Life isn't a rehearsal so make the most of what you've got*. He muttered, "I guess so."

Wiping her hands on a rag, Kate added, "But you haven't come down to see me. You've come to see that." She pointed towards the nearest car. "It's a modified Jaguar. A much modified Jaguar. An awesome piece of work."

Jordan stared at Kate, Angel and the sports car in turn.

Angel said, "Well, you've got to get around somehow. And, given what's happened, I thought it'd be better to put a bit of distance between you and Winter. Kate's your new handler. And driving instructor."

"I'll just get out of these overalls," she said, "and we can go for a spin. Okay?"

Jordan nodded eagerly. "More than okay."

"We'll have to stop somewhere and buy L-plates." Kate paused and added, "I feel like a Unit Red learner as well."

Jordan wasn't really listening. He ran his left hand along the roof of the Jaguar. It felt solid and sleek. It wasn't a dream. It was as real as his strange new life in Unit Red.

As one of Angel's agents, Jordan had immense power

and privilege, but he would also face immense danger and difficulty. He accepted it, though, because there was no other way forward. He accepted that he was part-human, part-machine because there was no tolerable alternative. He also accepted that there would be more enhancements to come. He might even look forward to them.

"Can I get in?"

"Sure," Angel replied. "Try out the driver's seat."

Jordan slipped inside and took a deep breath. The car smelled of new leather. It also oozed style and energy. He put his feet on the pedals and his hands on the steering wheel – and he smiled.

AUTHOR'S NOTE

In August 1944, an American ship carrying a large supply of bombs arrived in Sheerness, near London, to help with the war effort. Unfortunately, strong winds pushed the SS *Richard Montgomery* onto a sandbank in the River Thames where it broke its back. It is still there today, two-and-a-half kilometres from Sheerness and eight kilometres from Southend, with a cargo of 1400 tonnes of explosives. The wreck lies in about 15 metres of water, partly buried in silt. Successive British governments have not dared to risk moving it or do anything about it because it is disintegrating and some of the explosives are dangerously unstable. If one bomb exploded, it would set off the rest and the resulting blast would be one of the world's biggest non-nuclear explosions.

The bombs could be triggered if another ship rammed the wreck; a rusted piece of the remains collapsed onto the cargo; the tide pushed one bomb against another; a terrorist or criminal deliberately disturbed the shipment, or even if one of the fused bombs reacted spontaneously. If it happened, a column of water about 300 metres in diameter would be blown three kilometres into the sky. The blast would cause widespread damage in the area of the Thames Estuary, just sixty kilometres from central London. The towns of Sheerness and Southend and nearby oil and gas refineries would suffer the most. Forty thousand people would be affected. Among them, there would be some injuries and deaths.

MALCOLM ROSE ON THE SCIENCE BEHIND JORDAN STRYKER

When I want to come up with a new idea for a story, I usually look to science because scientists are always discovering and creating new things. Some exciting advances are bound to be just around the corner. For a few years, I have been keeping an eye on the coming bionic age. There are so many new developments I'm fascinated by: brain implants that give vision to the blind and hearing to the deaf, robotic limbs controlled entirely by the mind, touch-sensitive skin for artificial hands, designer DNA, power-enhancing drugs, developing replacement body parts through stem cells, terahertz technology, a bat-like echolocation device to help the blind, generating electricity from body movement, smart clothing, and drugs to wipe painful memories. It's clear that human re-engineering is under way.

Some of these body enhancements are already hitting the news. When soldiers return from war zones with dreadful injuries – often missing a limb after an encounter with a bomb – their medical treatment can grab the headlines. In writing the Jordan Stryker thriller series, I've been inspired not only by what modern medicine and technology can do for people, but also by their determination to cope.

I have seen today's artificial arms in action. By the power of thought alone, they can hold food, stir tea and pick up a small key. Whilst this cutting-edge science enables the disabled, it does not allow them to bust through doors like Jordan does with his bionic arm. In creating Jordan Stryker, I have not limited myself to today's exact medical technology. I have allowed myself to imagine where the science of body enhancement might take us in the next twenty years or so. By then, there will be some amazing developments. I've simply allowed Jordan to have the technology right now. I've also given him some of the grit shown by real-life victims of serious injury.

I haven't given Jordan the fantastic powers of a superhero. That would have been interesting and exciting, but not what I wanted to write about. If Jordan walks up a wall (and he might in a future book), it's because super-grip shoes are on the way to becoming practical, not because he's transforming into a superhero.

At least one expert thinks the first bionic eyes will be developed by 2020. Of all Jordan's abilities, I have peered into the future most with his artificial eyesight. I suspect that the power and range of his fictional vision will not become reality for many years.

One scientist is already talking about a time when people will merge with machines. This would be called the singularity. I don't know if that will happen and, if so, I wonder if it is to be welcomed or feared. If a human being and a machine become a single thing at some point, the hybrid will probably be really smart and live for ever. This seems too fanciful for Jordan, but I wouldn't be surprised if a character in the second book regards Jordan as a step on the way to this awesome future.

**LOOK OUT FOR
JORDAN STRYKER'S NEXT MISSION,
COMING SOON...**

ABOUT THE AUTHOR

Malcolm Rose was born in Coventry and began his career as a research scientist. He started writing stories while studying for his DPhil degree in chemistry, as a means of escape from everyday life. He is now a full-time writer best known for his gripping science-based thrillers and forensic crime series. He has been awarded the Angus Book Award twice and the Lancashire Children's Book of the Year. His novel, *Kiss of Death*, was chosen for the national Booked Up reading scheme, and was shortlisted for four prizes, including the Salisbury Schools' Book Award.

For more information about Malcolm Rose visit his website: www.malcolmrose.co.uk

To find out more about the Jordan Stryker series visit: www.usborne.com/jordanstryker

Also by MALCOLM ROSE

FORBIDDEN ISLAND

Mike and his friends ignore the clear warning sign on the island and decide to explore, not knowing just how dangerous it will turn out to be. As they stumble across a deadly secret, they realize they are alone in a race against time…before they become the island's next victims.

Enter a world of conspiracy and cover-ups in this brilliant mystery.

"A complex and chilling thriller…this pacy read asks uncomfortable questions."
The Daily Mail

ISBN 9780746098639

KISS OF DEATH

On a school trip to the plague village of Eyam, Seth is moved by the story of how villagers sacrificed their lives to the Black Death. Kim and Wes are more interested in what they see at the bottom of the wishing well – money!

But when they snatch the coins they also pick up something they hadn't bargained for, and as the hideous consequences of their theft catch up with them all, Seth is forced to face a terrifying truth. Has Eyam's plague-ridden past resurfaced to seek revenge?

"Fast-paced, full of nail-biting moments and more than one shock – not for the squeamish."
Primary Times

ISBN 9780746070642

THE TORTURED WOOD

Dillon is struggling to make friends at his new school, and he begins to suspect there's something rotten at the core of the tightknit community, something they're trying to hide.

He finds refuge in the wood that seems to be at the very heart of the mystery. Will the wood give up its dark secret, or is Dillon being drawn into a trap?

Eerie and atmospheric, *The Tortured Wood* is a thriller with a sting in the tale.

"A gripping story... Good spooky stuff."
Adèle Geras, *TES*

ISBN 9780746077436

FOR MORE SPINE-CHILLING STORIES,
CHECK OUT
WWW.FICTION.USBORNE.COM